BULLETPROOF HEART

Corralling the Cowboy (Book 1)

Cornering the Cowgirl (Book 2)

BULLETPROOF HEART

A BILLIONAIRE COWBOY ROMANTIC SUSPENSE NOVEL

KATIE O'CONNOR

SNARKY HEART PRESS

Published February 2020
(katieohwrites.com)

ISBN: 978-1-989816-00-4 (Kindle Edition)
ISBN: 978-1-989816-01-1 (Other Digital Editions)
ISBN: 978-1-989816-02-8 (Print Edition)

Design and cover art by Jenn Howard
Formatting by Shelley Kassian

DEDICATION

In a world full of people, kind and otherwise, certain individuals stand out more than others. This novel was conceived during one of my endless, monthly, drug infusions to control my rheumatoid arthritis. It seems fitting that I dedicate this story to the lovely nurses, aides and support staff in Day Medicine at Calgary's South Health Campus. They treat me with care and respect and pretend to enjoy my irreverent humor. They make a tough day better, every single time. Without them, I would be unable to walk without a cane. There aren't adequate words to express my gratitude, so I offer this simple thank you.

ACKNOWLEDGMENTS

Countless hands were involved in the creation of this book. I have a wonderful team surrounding me. My beastie (or bestie if you prefer), Linda, fires ideas at me faster than I can write them and is fabulous at finding gaping plot holes.

As always, my critique partners have been invaluable.

Special thanks go out to The Write Chicks, my newly formed romance writing group. Cheers to you ladies for helping me keep it real and knocking me down when I needed it.

Extra thanks to Author Jan O'Hara for coming up with a title I struggled to find.

CHAPTER ONE

*A*pril Cooper spared a quick glance at the swollen gray clouds as the rain poured down in buckets. It should have been a relief, but it wasn't. It annoyed her. Too much, too fast and maybe even too late! She slammed her hand on the steering wheel. Dammit, she didn't need this.

Wildwood, Alberta, was experiencing its hottest, driest summer in a decade. Crops that should have been thigh high were barely to the knee. Farmers and ranchers needed rain, desperately. But not all at once. Not in the span of an hour. The earth was dirty-thirties parched, the ground cracked and broken and wouldn't absorb the moisture quickly enough. Too much of it would simply run off and drain away into the ditches or flood the low-lying areas. What they needed was a week of light, misty, easily absorbed rain.

She'd been optimistic that they'd get a sprinkle when she headed to town for groceries and chicken feed, now, her hopes were crushed. Another dream down the drain, just like her dream to advance to charge nurse of day medicine at Calgary South Health Campus. That aspiration exploded in her face like a cheap firecracker when she was falsely accused of theft and terminated. With nothing left, she'd fled the city, seeking sanctuary on her grandfather's ranch. The ranch was supposed to bring peace and comfort, and a safe place to land. Instead, it came with a manure load of problems she had no idea how to handle.

In the thirty seconds between the feed store and the ranch's rust bucket truck, April Cooper was drenched to the bone. Now, forty-five minutes into a twenty-minute ride, she was shivering uncontrollably and her bladder was fit to burst. If this drenching made her sick or endangered her baby, she didn't know what she'd do.

She had to pee. Oh Lord, she needed to use the bathroom. How could being four months pregnant shrink her bladder so drastically? She was barely even showing yet. Mother Nature continued to dump gallons of water and the bald truck tires were starting to hydroplane on the standing water of the highway. She splashed through a particularly low spot, swerving uncontrollably until she passed through the puddle. Her sigh of relief was short-lived when the stupid truck shuddered and stalled. She coasted to the side of Highway 16 and flipped on her hazard lights. At least those still worked.

The sky lit with repeated flashes of sheet lightning and thunder boomed, shaking her truck and making her ears throb.

"Crap in a basket," she muttered. "I don't need this. Not now. Come on, Bessy girl." She slipped the truck into neutral, pushed in the clutch and turned the key. "Don't let me down now."

Nothing.

Not a squeak, not a groan and certainly not the roar of her engine flaring to life. She closed her eyes and prayed for patience before trying again.

Nothing.

She pulled out her cell phone to discover there was no service. She wasn't surprised; reception in this area was spotty on a good day; in the middle of a thunderstorm, it was nonexistent. And she still needed to pee. She wasn't getting out in this monsoon. She searched the floorboards, in vain, for an empty container of some sort that she might be able to convert into a makeshift bathroom. There wasn't a single thing on the floor; not even a throw away coffee cup. What farm truck didn't have empty containers in it? She tried the backseat. Nothing under the groceries or the cooler she'd loaded earlier.

There *was* an old rain slicker. Full of holes and mouse chewed, but it would cover her while she was out of the truck. She couldn't wait any longer; she had to go. Now.

She peered out the windows, checked for traffic and slipped into the jacket, choking back a gag at its musty, oily smell. Her stomach clenched; it was way too sensitive these days. She climbed gingerly down from the truck and raced around to the passenger side, dropped her pants and squatted.

She had barely started when the sound of a vehicle penetrated the storm.

"Just keep going," she muttered. "Don't stop." Oh, God, if someone saw her, she'd die of embarrassment.

April sighed as the vehicle came to a halt behind her. A door slammed. Fate was against her today.

"Need a hand," a strong masculine voice called out.

"Don't come any closer." She tried to squeeze the flow to a stop.

"What?"

"Hang on. Don't come any closer," she called over her shoulder. Sweet heaven, don't let this stranger see her with her butt hanging out on the edge of the road in the middle of a monsoon. If this were a sitcom, it would be funny, but now it was mortifying. Thankfully, the slicker was long enough it protected her privacy somewhat.

Finished, she yanked up her jeans, dropped her shirt and turned to face the voice. The man standing beside an old GMC pickup seemed tall and solid. Somehow his suit was reassuring. Crazy people didn't wear suits, did they? She ignored the embarrassing heat that flooded her face. Thankfully, he had enough courtesy to avoid mentioning the fact she'd been addressing the call of nature when he arrived.

"Is everything okay?" he called out.

"Um, my truck died after skidding through that lake back there. I can't get it to start."

"It's a crappy day to be stuck in the rain." He approached slowly until they stood six feet apart, facing each other, on the driver's side of her truck. She backed up three steps, keeping her distance. No sense getting too close to a stranger.

Glory be; he was tall. At five six, she wasn't short, but he had to have eight inches on her. The rain rapidly flattened his sandy brown hair, turning it dark and slowly taking the waves out of it. His face wreathed in a reassuring grin and his dark blue eyes sparkled in the dim light of early afternoon.

"You should have a rain jacket on." Heat rose in her face. Why had she chastised a man she'd never met?

"I forgot to pack it. I'll pick one up later, if this crazy

weather continues." He shrugged off her concern. "Is it okay if I give it a try?"

"Give what a try?" She blinked at him in confusion.

"The truck. Is it okay if I try to start her up?"

Did she want some random man starting her truck? What if he stole it and abandoned her here? The thought was ridiculous, it probably wouldn't start for him either. "Oh, yes. Go ahead. She's not going anywhere anyway. It's not like you could steal her since she won't start. Not that you'd want to steal a piece of junk like this. Um, not that I think you'd steal it…" She rambled to a stop, she sounded foolish blathering on like this.

He quirked one eyebrow at her. "Nervous?"

"Oh crap. I'm babbling. Aren't I? I usually do when I'm nervous. Not that you make me nervous. I'm just tired of being out in the rain."

The eyebrow quirked again.

The flow of words stammered to a halt.

"I'm Wade Kelly." He climbed into the cab. He tried to start it, popped the hood and climbed back out a moment later. "Well, she's not going to start. I'll check if there's anything obviously wrong with the engine." He stepped around, walking toward the hood.

"Good grief, man, you'll ruin that suit. Get back in your truck. The rain will stop soon. And cell reception will come back."

"Don't worry about the suit. I've got another one." He chuckled.

"You don't have to do this." She followed him to the front of the truck.

"So, I should leave a damsel in distress stranded on the

side of the road? Sorry, princess, that's not in my repertoire of tricks."

The wind ripped the raincoat hood off her head and the rain redoubled its efforts to drown her. She swiped her sodden hair off her face; the old jacket was more of a sieve than a weather block; she was drenched anyway, why worry about it now?

He lifted the truck hood and poked around the engine. "I don't suppose you have any tools in this death trap? Do you?"

"Not a one, sorry." Death trap? Yeah, the truck was a beater, but it was hardly a death trap. He had his nerve. She bit back a snide remark. He was trying to help.

"There's nothing I can do without tools. By the looks of things, there could be a hundred things wrong, but it's probably just old age." He slammed the hood shut. "This old girl needs a mechanic or, better yet, a trip to the bone yard. What is she an eight-two?"

"Eighty-four, I think. Does it matter?"

"No, not really. But with a lot of TLC, she'd be a grand dame again."

"Unfortunately, I don't have that kind of time, or money. And if I did, she'd be replaced with something a little more reliable." April sighed. "Thanks for the help. I'll just sit and wait for the storm to pass."

"Don't be silly. I'll give you a ride home, or back to town, if you prefer."

"No thanks. I'll wait it out." Is he nuts? Does he really think I'd hitch a ride with a stranger? Maybe he wasn't as nice as he looked; maybe he had an ulterior motive. Serial killers looked like regular people, didn't they? Great, now her overactive imagination was kicking in.

"Come on, princess, how far can it be?"

"It's not far, but I don't know you."

"True enough. But I haven't ravaged you, yet."

She stared at him, slack jawed. "I didn't think that…" Holy crap, he could read her mind. This was bad.

"Of course, you did. A beautiful woman, alone on the side of a deserted road. It crossed your mind before you were done with your business." He winked.

"I can't believe you mentioned *that*," she gasped. *Beautiful? Now he was trying to butter her up?* As much as the compliment surprised her, it pleased her as well.

"Well, it's hardly a secret between us. And I didn't see anything important. Climb into my truck. You're frozen right through and I've got heat," he sing-songed and waved toward his pickup.

She stared at him; knowing she shouldn't take a ride from a stranger. He seemed like a nice guy. She bit her lip. Should she accept a ride and get out of this crappy weather? She would be risking her life and her baby's. Then again, she was risking the baby's life by hanging around, freezing her ass off. "Sold." Shivering from the cold, she pivoted toward his vehicle. She felt his stare on her back as she walked away.

CHAPTER TWO

*W*ade studied her as she walked away. Funny she didn't wait after she made up her mind. The woman had spunk, that was for sure. And she was pretty, as well as feisty. Even if she was stick-skinny. Her long blonde hair hung limp around her face, sodden with the downpour. What little he could see under that ridiculous jacket was all angles and curves. She could use a little meat on her bones, that's for sure. Why did women think you needed to be under-weight to be attractive? It bothered him that too many socialites felt you couldn't be thin enough or rich enough. That was one of the factors that instigated this…sabbatical. That and his desire to find a farm or ranch to created a rural retreat for himself. The crazy, skinny women chasing him for his money were adding to his already disabling burden of running an oilfield servicing business in a dwindling economy.

He reached into her truck and grabbed the purse he'd seen on the seat earlier, locked the doors and climbed into his fully restored, vintage 1972 GMC pickup. This truck was the only woman in his life, and he intended to keep it that way.

"Here are the keys and your purse. I didn't think you'd want to leave them behind. I locked her up."

"Oh my gosh. I can't believe I forgot my purse. Thanks for bringing it. I need to get more sleep."

"Now, where to, princess?" She was cute, pretty in a casual way, but she seemed a bit scatterbrained. It didn't matter, she needed a ride and he wouldn't leave a woman stranded on the side of the road.

"April," she corrected him.

"This…is a truck, not a time machine. I can neither take you back to last April nor take you forward to next year." He chuckled.

The tension eased from her shoulders and she laughed with him. "I meant my name is April."

"I got that. I just thought you looked a mite nervous and I'd lighten things up a bit. Relax, I'm not going to bite you." Even if the idea did hold a certain undeniable appeal. Man, he'd like to taste those glistening pink lips.

She was shivering like a leaf in a windstorm. He cranked the truck to life and heat blasted from the dash and floorboards.

"All right, Princess April, where can I take you? And before you argue about it, there's no sense sitting here half the day waiting for the rain to stop. You might as well be home and warm. Or back in town, if that's where you came from."

He could almost see the thoughts scrambling around in her head. She was wary, rightly so, but she looked frozen to the bone. Safety probably battled comfort for supremacy behind those liquid chocolate eyes. Obviously, she didn't know who he was or she'd know she was safe. He was tickled by the anonymity; this had to be the first time in five years his wealthy reputation didn't precede him. A lovely girl next to him who didn't recognize him made the day special; he didn't even care about the torrential downpour hammering them; or the potential delay of his plans.

"Look, you're already in my truck. I'll give you a ride home or back to town and leave you be. Although, it would be nice if you loaned me a towel to dry off with. Who knew a wool suit could soak up so much water?" He struggled out of the jacket and folded it on the seat between them, waiting for a response.

After several long minutes of warming her hands in front of the blowing heater, she seemed to reach a decision. "The ranch is about six miles from here. Straight ahead three miles then turn left."

A quick shoulder check and they were on their way, westbound.

"Slip out of that jacket. It's probably blocking the heat. You'll warm up faster that way. And I expect you're dry under it," he advised.

"You'd think so, wouldn't you?" She chuckled lamely and slid out of it. "But this thing has more holes than cheesecloth and I'm soaked through."

Her scoop-necked T-shirt clung to her minimal curves and he had to struggle to keep his eyes on the road and off her. How weird was that? He, Wade Kelly Borne, known throughout the province for his penchant for luxuriously upholstered women, was fixated on the skinniest woman he'd seen for months. He ignored the stirring in his groin when she lifted her arms to push her hair back, causing her shirt to tighten even farther. This was bad. He had a job to do, and it did not involve getting tangled up with a woman, any woman.

"You might consider investing in a better jacket," he suggested.

"I have a better one, but it was sunny and hot when I left this morning. I wasn't expecting rain. All month it's been threatening to storm, but the clouds seemed to skirt by us and dump water everywhere else, like Saskatchewan. Although, the radio tells me the whole area is socked in for a long, hard rain. I found this pathetic excuse for a coat in the truck when I stopped to…"

He chuckled. It was cute that bodily functions made her uncomfortable.

"You found it in the truck? Isn't it yours?"

"Well, yes and no. And sort of."

"That clears things up perfectly." She wasn't very forthcoming, she seemed to be hiding something from him. She was rapidly becoming a puzzle he wanted to figure out, and not in a good way. He didn't have time for deceit or hidden agendas.

"Turn at the next left," she advised. "The truck belongs to the ranch and I'm sort of taking care of things for a while."

Another cryptic response. He followed her instruction and turned left down a gravel road and a short distance later crossed the eastbound lanes of Highway 16. He drove down the rough road carefully avoiding the puddles she warned were always deep.

Turning right again, they crossed a Texas gate and drove under a faded sign declaring the land to be the Lazy-W Ranch. He did a double take at the sign. Part of his mission, on his work trip, vacation combo was to scout out the Lazy-W as a potential investment. The rumor mill told him the ranch was in financial straits and could end up on the market. If it was what he was looking for, he intended to scoop it up before it was officially for sale. He hadn't expected to arrive in this fashion, he'd intended to keep his surveillance subtle. Rescuing a member of the ranch staff was definitely not on the agenda.

A road, of sorts, crossed a cow-mowed field and wandered past a fenced-in equipment yard complete with shop. Dozens of cows grazed peacefully on both sides of the road, oblivious to the weather. A large broken-down, but still useable, barn, a stable and a series of corrals sat on the left-hand side of the path. The gravel lane led upward into a patch of trees.

"Up that small hill, please. And stop in front of the big house."

"The big house," he teased. "I thought you said ranch, not plantation."

"You'll understand it when we clear the bush."

They passed through a couple hundred feet of old growth forest, the underbrush stomped and chewed flat by cattle. They crested the hill and crossed another Texas gate into an enormous yard. To the left was a long thin house designed to look like a cabin, but with several dormer windows across the roofline. On the far side of the yard were half a dozen small buildings laid out like one side of a street in an old western town. Each building had a name on a plaque hanging from the rafters. Hotel, Saloon, Jail, Bathhouse, Livery and several others faded to near invisibility.

"The hotel is actually a bunkhouse." She pointed to the largest building at the south end of the row. "My grandfather thought it would look cute if the guest cabins looked like an old west town. Bed and breakfast clients used to love it. Unfortunately, things are a bit rundown now."

A bit? The place looked like it should be torched. The grass was little more than mud and the boardwalk along the front of the cabins was warped and twisted; clearly a tripping hazard. The dilapidated state of everything would drop the market value substantially. The *big house* wasn't big at all. It seemed like a modest family home but, in relation to the old west buildings, it was large.

"It's okay to drive on the grass," she advised him. "Pull right up to the front porch."

He pulled to a stop as a grizzled old man in a tattered straw cowboy hat stepped gingerly out onto the porch to stand sheltered from the pounding rain by the overhang.

"Come inside." She glanced at Wade and jumped out of the truck.

Her sudden acceptance left him feeling pole-axed and more than a little guilty about scoping the place out. He shrugged off the guilt, this was business and if helping April led him to better information, or maybe a deal, that's just how it is. Half a moment later he followed her onto the porch.

"Missy, I figured you were lost for sure. Where's the truck? And who's this city slicker." He waved dismissively in Wade's direction.

"Bessy died," she replied. "We can use the tractor to tow her home later. This is Wade. He rescued me and gave me a ride. Wade, this old geezer is Jack, the ranch foreman."

"I ain't old," he groused.

"You were old when I was a girl. You're practically ancient now." She kissed his whiskered cheek tenderly. "But I'd be lost without you. If you hadn't found me when you did, I'd be homeless as well as jobless." She hugged him tightly.

Homeless and jobless? There must be a story here. Wade's curiosity peaked further.

A golden-red, knee-high dog hopped up the steps on three legs, sliding with each hop. It scurried to April's feet and woofed softly.

She leaned down to pat it. "Hey, Biscuit. Girl, you should be inside, not hanging outside in the rain. You'll catch cold."

"Biscuit?" Wade asked. Crazy name for a dog, but from what he gathered, April was…unconventional.

"Grampa had a thing for food names. Biscuit here is the best danged cattle dog for miles around. On three legs she can outwork almost every other dog in the area." April kneeled and tussled with the dog for a moment. "Now shoo, go find someplace warm to rest." Biscuit scurried off to lie on a blanket under a chair on the far end of the porch.

"Would it be okay if I brought my suitcase in, just long enough to change before I hit the road?" His body temperature was dropping, he wanted nothing more than to get out of these clothes, and finish the job he'd come to do.

Jack pinned him with a glare that felt like a physical blow. "You mind your manners, mister. Don't be getting any ideas about my April or you'll answer to me."

Jack was old and frail and Wade didn't doubt for one second the old guy would try to take him out if he felt the need; even if it was a battle the old timer was destined to lose.

"No, sir. I'll be on my best behavior. I'll change, and then I'll be gone."

"Nonsense," April grasped his arm, the chill of her hand

through his shirtsleeve sent heat racing through him. "You'll stay for coffee, at least, and maybe lunch too."

"I should be going. But I'd love a coffee if it's not too much trouble." Excellent, he had an open invitation to look around, scope things out.

"No trouble at all. I'll start the coffee and then get changed. Get your bag and come inside." She stepped through the wood-framed screen door, closing it gently behind her.

"Watch yourself, boy," Jack warned. "I'm not putting up with any shenanigans. Tell April I'm moving that last bred heifer into the barn. She's due any minute and no sense in letting the calf catch a chill. But I won't be long, mark my words." He shook a boney finger in Wade's face.

"What's a bred heifer?" Wade asked.

"Danged city slickers. A heifer's a female cow that ain't had a calf. A bred heifer is having her first. After that she's just a cow." There was something in Jack's tone that implied Wade had somehow redeemed himself by admitting his ignorance about cattle.

Jack snatched a heavy green slicker off a wall hook and slid into it, and then ambled around the corner, a hitch in his gait slowing his steps.

Wade inhaled deeply and a weight seemed to lift off his shoulders. The view and the smell of rain reminded him of the time his foster parents had taken him and his sister to visit a cowboy ranch in Saskatchewan when he was fourteen. It was one of his favorite memories, the horses, the cows, the trail rides; it had all been so peaceful and for years afterward, the child he'd been had dreamed of being a cowboy. But life drifted by and his had taken another direction. Living in

Alberta, he'd been drawn to the oil patch as if pulled by forces beyond his control. He made his fortune in the petroleum industry, but he did miss rural life and someday hoped to retire to the country.

Wade stood on the porch for a moment, looking around the yard. The Lazy-W Ranch must have been impressive at some point, although its glory had faded and aged. In an instant, he could see the ranch as it had been and what it could be with the right man behind the reins. He grunted at the fanciful thought; it didn't matter what it was, or what it could be. He'd heard this place might be coming up for sale and had come to see if they could turn it into a corporate retreat. There was huge money in retreats and he was always looking for a good investment. Not that he'd mention that to April. Or maybe he'd buy it for his own use.

CHAPTER THREE

*A*pril hurried inside and started the coffee before racing to her attic room to towel off and change. She dried hastily, ran a brush through her hair and slipped into jeans and a warm sweater. Downstairs, she tossed her clothing into the dryer and headed back into the living room.

Wade stood indecisively, dripping water on the mat.

"What are you doing?" she chided. "Don't just stand there. Get out of those fancy shoes and come inside." He must be crazy to stay there, drenched.

She led him to the bathroom and handed him a towel. "I'll be in the kitchen when you're changed." She pointed down the hallway to the other end of the house and left him standing in the bathroom.

She loved this place. When she'd first visited as a child, she fell in love with the unconventional layout. With the living room at one end, facing west, and the kitchen at the other, facing east, there was a perfect place to relax any time of the day. In between were a bathroom and utility room and three moderately sized bedrooms, one of which had been converted to an office-library combination. Upstairs, the attic had been divided into a couple of bedrooms and an open living area. Dormer windows provided light. Boxes of fabric and supplies stood stacked in one of the attic rooms, waiting for April to have a chance to unpack them and renew her addiction to quilting. But that would have to wait; there was too much ranch work to do to be bothered with trifles like hobbies; even if she did want to get started on a baby quilt.

She busied herself in the spacious kitchen, setting out coffee mugs, sugar and a plate full of cookies. She rummaged in the fridge for the jar of fresh cream from a neighbor who raised dairy cows.

"This is a great house," he declared. "How old is it?"

She jerked back out of the avocado green fridge, slamming her head into the bottom of the freezer door handle. "Shoot." She groaned and rubbed her head. "You startled me. Didn't anyone ever tell you not to sneak up on a person?"

"Sorry. I got excited. I love this house. I peeked into the open rooms. I hope that's okay." He winced as if realizing he might have overstepped his bounds.

"It's fine. If it wasn't, I'd have shut the doors. No secrets here." It was her turn to wince at the slight untruth of her words as she set the cream on the table. "The ranch was founded in eighteen eighty-two, before the Grand Trunk Pacific Railway came through Wildwood. Though it wasn't called Wildwood then. It was called Junkins, which is a really stupid name for a town." She chuckled. "But the original house burned down in nineteen thirty-nine. This one was finished in nineteen forty."

She studied Wade as he glanced around the enormous

kitchen. A charming, homey, scarred and chipped pine table dominated the room. Twelve chairs surrounded it and it could be expanded further. An ancient cuckoo clock hung on the faded yellow wall alongside a large collection of rough wood framed photos of the ranch. A pot of yellow flowers sat in the window, smiling happily in the sun.

"Are those dandelions?"

"What can I say?" She loved how he sounded shocked. "I love dandelions."

"The house has had some upgrades then?" he asked, seeming to accept her love of the yellow weeds.

"Some. In the mid-eighties. But she needs plenty more work. Things are starting to fail. I haven't begun repairs yet and don't know when I will, but I've started the list."

"They're probably mostly cosmetic. The house is upright and stable. She looks like she has good bones, though she's probably short on insulation and needs new appliances." He waved at the outdated fridge and stove.

"And a new furnace, someday," April said wistfully. "Thankfully, there's still a wood stove for heat."

"You've lived here all your life?"

Strangely, the question didn't feel rude or intrusive. He just sounded curious.

"I wish. I visited here almost every summer until I was fourteen. I wasn't lucky enough to live here full time. My father had other ideas and wanted nothing to do with the ranch. Do you want a tour of the house?" Her offer must have surprised him as much as it did her, he hesitated before answering.

"I'd love one."

"Follow me. This is the kitchen." She waved around the

room. "That door opens to the covered back deck, the best place, ever, for drinking my morning coffee. It's quiet and peaceful, and we often get elk, whitetail or mule deer grazing on the lawn."

Muted sounds of cursing came down the hallway, growing louder as Jack approached. "No good rotten bastards done it again."

Her hands flew to her mouth. "Oh no, what this time."

"Red's dead."

"Who's Red?" Wade blurted.

"One of the three remaining bulls," April moaned. A tear ran down her cheek. "We can't survive another season with only two bulls. There isn't enough semen stored to inseminate the remaining cows and keep the bloodlines clean." She leaned on the table for support, her knees weak and head spinning. Not another crisis.

"The rotten bastards shot him square between the eyes." Jack dropped into a kitchen chair, cradling his head in his hands. "We can't stand another blow like this. There's no way we'll ever get this place back on track if crap like this keeps happening."

"I'll call the RCMP. The rain's tapered off. Maybe they can make it out." April picked up the phone and punched in the local Royal Canadian Mounted Police detachment's phone number.

"Fat lotta good that'll do. Frank Miller's got it in for this place. Don't know why, but he's bound and determined to shut us down. He's been in a foul mood for months. I heard rumors that even his staff are rebelling against him. There's talk of him losing control of the precinct." Jack fell silent while she talked on the phone.

"They'll be out as soon as they deal with the accidents caused by the storm," she sighed and hung up. "We might as well have coffee while we wait. It's sixty kilometers to the detachment and they're busy. Millie, the receptionist, said not to touch anything."

"The rain will destroy any evidence," Wade said, picking up the coffeepot and pouring them each a generous mug, looking as if he belonged in the kitchen. Obviously, he was a man used to being in charge.

April dropped dejectedly into a chair and Wade eased into the one beside her.

Gently, he touched her arm. "It'll be okay."

"How is it going to be okay? It's not a coincidence. Someone is out to get us." She tried to ignore the comforting warmth of his touch. He was a stranger, it shouldn't make her feel better, but it did. It was nice to have someone in her corner for a change.

"What does that mean? Explain it to me." He stirred cream and sugar into his coffee.

"Might as well," Jack declared, sharing a glance with April. "If he was part of the bastards hounding us, he'd never have given you a ride home."

"Unless I was trying to mislead you and win your confidence," Wade piped up.

"Are you?" she asked, suddenly back to questioning his credentials. Maybe he wasn't a knight on a white charger, maybe he was the villain.

"Princess, if I were, I sure wouldn't tell you. I'd just bide my time and do my damage. Be reasonable here. Look at me. Do I look like someone out to destroy you?" He waved at his pristine white button-down shirt and neatly pressed dress pants.

She studied him from head to toe. His dry clothes were a step down from his designer suit but hardly ranch casual. Even his socks looked expensive. He looked like a displaced city-boy, not a rural ruffian.

"I guess not." Not that she'd know what a saboteur looked like, except that he'd probably choose clothing to blend in, not stand out like a fox in a chicken coop.

"So, fill me in. Maybe I can come up with an idea that you haven't. We can brainstorm your troubles."

"I'll let Jack explain. It started long before I got here." As she said the words, she realized that, for whatever reason, Wade seemed trustworthy. She mentally shrugged off her easy acceptance of him; typically, she was more cautious.

CHAPTER FOUR

Wade watched Jack take a long swallow of his coffee.

"I swear to god, if this were any other ranch, and you were anyone else, I'll pack my bags and leave. It's dangerous here. Someone is going to get hurt. Or shot. Or worse." Jack sucked in an angry breath. "I'll tell you one thing, I'm sick to death of everything that's going wrong around here. Red's murder is about the last straw. Who in their right mind shoots someone else's bull? I swear to God, this is a threat. Someone is trying to scare us off this place and I don't know why." He slammed his fist onto the table, rattling their mugs.

Seriously? Wade looked back and forth between April and Jack. They looked shaken, but not terrified. They should be freaked out. There must be more to this than they let on. One thing for sure, he'd need to solve the mystery of what was happening here, before he decided if this was the right property to purchase.

Jack took a deep breath and began again. "About ten years

ago, April's grandfather, Morgan Wyatt, was still alive and this place was hopping."

"Morgan Wyatt? Seriously?" Wade blurted out, momentarily distracted from his plan to investigate everything happening at the Lazy-W.

"Morgan's daddy, that'd be April's great-granddaddy, loved all things western and all things cowboy. He particularly loved them Earps. Wyatt's a family name. You gonna let me tell this without interrupting?" The old man glared at him.

"Sorry, it's almost unbelievable." A ranching family named Wyatt? He'd never have guessed that one, except maybe as a joke. The universe sure had a sense of humor. He was tempted to laugh aloud, only the fear of offending them kept his mirth silent.

"It is at that, isn't it?" April chimed in. "As a girl, I read everything I could find about the OK Corral. I could show you the family Bible with birth records and the names all the way back to the eighteen fifties."

Wade held up his hands. "No need. I'll take your word for it. It just surprised me. Go on." He gestured toward Jack, who swilled half a mug of coffee before continuing.

"Ten years ago, Morgan was running this place. One of the biggest cattle operations in the area. Hugely successful with folks coming from all around to buy our cows and our bull semen. Morgan had two children. April's daddy, Justin, and his older brother, John. Justin never did like the ranch, or work of any kind. He hightailed it out of here as soon as he graduated from high school. And John left home as a teenager, working on the rigs when the urge, or financial necessity, stuck him. Thought he was going to make a fortune as a rig hand." He took another glug of coffee and swallowed it loudly. The man's table manners were atrocious.

"So, 'bout six years ago, like the prodigal son, John Wyatt showed up outta the blue. Drunk. Dirt poor. That boy's always been full of trouble. Right from the start, he was looking for a fight and kicking up shit."

"So, you think he's behind this?" Wade queried.

Jack glared and Wade leaned back, miming zipping his lips. Apparently, you couldn't rush a good story.

"Couple years later, Morgan got sick. Some kind of wasting disease. Doc never did figure out what caused it. He just wasted away, all slow and painful like. April's granddaddy, Morgan, died in two thousand ten."

Pain and sadness washed over April's face. She must have loved her grandfather deeply. She was still mourning him. By the sounds of things, her family had been burdened with more than their share of trouble over the years; weight like that could wear on a person's soul.

"John took over the running of things, but did a terrible job. Things started declining. 'Bout then, a couple hands got shot at while they rode the fence line. We lost a lot of good men; everyone started leaving; nobody wants to work in a place where bullets are whizzing by at random. John ran the place into the ground and disappeared a year ago. So, I started searching for Missy, here. She's the last rightful heir with her daddy gone too. I lost contact when she stopped coming around after her grandfather passed."

"He found me and I came home mid-May. Good timing too, because I was in a bit of a tough spot."

She must be referring to the homeless and jobless comment she'd made earlier. Gears turned in his head. This was one messed-up and confusing situation. "So, let me get this straight, there are questions about Morgan's death and John's disappearance, and the RCMP have it in for you. They're probably all related in some fashion."

"And don't forget the rustling," a deep voice called from the porch.

April jumped to her feet, knocking her chair askew.

Wade rose to stand between her and the door. Her overreaction to the voice concerned him. The protector in him wouldn't stand by without defending her from the threat, real or imagined.

"Mind if I come in?"

"You know this guy?" Wade asked April and Jack, even though the man was clearly an RCMP officer. He was close to six foot six and the biggest, blackest man Wade had ever seen. He had tough and mean written all over him. Something in his eyes said tired and broken. Those things together could be a dangerous combination if he was power-hungry.

"And you are?" the officer questioned dryly.

"A family friend," Wade retorted, not liking the way the officer used his size to intimidate; it reeked of an under-appreciated authority pushing a private agenda.

"Come in," April invited warily. "Wade, this is Sergeant Franklin Miller, RCMP. Sergeant Miller, this is Wade. Did you want coffee?"

"Wade who?" Franklin stepped out of his boots. "You look familiar."

"Wade Kelly." Wade let the mistruth roll right off his tongue. "Shouldn't be familiar. I'm not from around here." Somehow, it seemed prudent to keep his full name, Wade Kelly

Borne, hidden for the time being. No sense letting on that he was a big name in the province's oil field. A good cop could link that back to his many investments and before long, they'd all know he was scouting for retreat space. Hiding who he was from strangers had become a habit, unless they recognized him. He was tired of being hounded, expected to commit to people's pet projects and nutjob schemes. As irritating as hearing about questionable business plans were, it had nothing on people introducing him to their eligible daughters.

Everyone stared at Wade, questions in their eyes. He pretended not to notice. "Jack and April have been filling me in on the history here. Sounds like some…unusual happenings. Do you have any leads? Any suspects?"

"Suspects in what? Hunting accidents? A sick old man? Another who got fed up with ranching and took off. There isn't anything to be suspicious of," Miller declared belligerently.

"What about the bull with the bullet in his brain? Hunting accident in July, no doubt," Wade growled. Couldn't Miller see that the coincidences and bad luck were piling up weirdly. Miller set his teeth on edge. Wade was skilled at reading people, and something didn't ring true here. There was more to this cop than met the eye.

"Do you have a problem with me?" Miller demanded.

"Honestly, I'm undecided. But these people, my friends, are scared and you don't seem to be taking it seriously. I've already had to rescue April once today. I'm not itching to face gunfire."

"You city folk, always thinking the worst."

"With a third of my bulls dead, I'm leaping to the worst

as well." April dumped her coffee down the sink. "Should we go look now?"

Wade admired the way she stuck up for herself and took control.

"Guess that'd be best," Miller agreed.

"Can I borrow a pair of rubber boots?" Wade asked. "I don't think my leather shoes will hold up well under all that water and mud." With Miller's bad attitude, there was no way Wade was going to pass up the chance to learn more about him. Wade ignored the idea that he might be feeling protective toward April. This was about protecting a potential investment, nothing more.

April found him boots and a tattered yellow slicker. They stomped, single file, down the hill to the bull pen and stood in the misty rain, staring at the deceased bull.

"Just happened," Jack declared. "He was fine this morning when I checked the barn. I found him just before we called you. He was dead, but still warm. Likely the thunder concealed the shots."

"I'll call the vet and get an autopsy done…bull-topsy? Whatever you want to call it. This isn't a hunting accident. This is malicious mischief at best and an outright threat at worst," Franklin declared. "You should keep an eye out for strangers. Maybe set a watch for a few days." He pulled out his cell phone and glanced at the screen before sliding it back into his pocket.

April nodded but didn't speak. Her beautiful brown eyes were shuttered, concealing her thoughts. Premonition ants marched up Wade's spine. This was going to get a whole lot worse before it got better. In that instant, he decided to stick around for a while, if they'd have him; because he didn't think they could handle this alone. A skinny, unsure woman and a rickety old man weren't much of a defense.

"I think I'll spend a few extra days of my vacation here," he piped up.

"What?" April gaped at him.

Turning his head so Miller couldn't see, Wade mimed silence.

Her eyes widened and narrowed as she stared at him.

"Oh, didn't you have plans?" She must have recognized what he was thinking. "No need to change them on my account." Her eyes held million dollars worth of questions and he was certain she would fire them at him the first chance she got. He looked forward to going head to head with her. She had an appealing, feisty spirit.

"Easily changeable. I didn't really have any. I was just escaping the city for a while. So, I'll just hang out for a day or two, unless you'd rather I didn't." He watched the expressions flitting over her face. Finally, she nodded her acceptance.

"I'll use the house phone to call the vet. Reception's crappy today," Miller said.

"Go ahead, I'll just take a minute alone with Red."

Obediently, Miller and Jack headed toward the house. Wade stepped away a few paces and waited quietly, watching as April leaned on the fence, talking to the deceased bull. He couldn't hear her words, but the tone was low and soothing. He wondered if she was comforting the bull or herself. She had to be frightened; her palms rubbed up and down her arms and she shifted from foot to foot. Her eyes darted anxiously around the yard. He didn't blame her; he was nervous himself and it took a lot to scare him.

CHAPTER FIVE

Slowly, April wiped the tears from her eyes. She'd only been back on the Lazy-W for two months and it was already the home her younger self had dreamed it would be. This was where she belonged and every fiber of her being loved it here. She'd let the pain of losing her grandfather bury her and stayed away too long. Losing Red felt like losing a beloved family member. She turned toward the house and discovered Wade standing a few feet behind her. "Oh, I thought you had left."

"I didn't think that would be wise. I was keeping watch. Miller said to be on guard and you seemed…distracted." His gaze flittered between her and the surrounding tree line.

"Why?" He was a stranger, yet seemed bent on helping her. She couldn't decide if that was weird or comforting. The jury was still out on whether or not to trust him. She crossed her arms and threw him a questioning glance.

"Why keep watch? Why hang around? That's easy, something's not right here, and I'll be damned if I'll let a woman stay alone with only a crippled old man for protection when taking a few days of my vacation time might mean the difference between life and death." His words rang strong and heartfelt.

"I don't even know you." She rubbed her arms as the wind picked up speed and roared across the clearing housing the bull pens. They were empty now. The light drizzle increased to a full-out downpour bringing back her earlier chill.

"True, you don't know me. Yet. I wouldn't feel right leaving you two alone. I don't expect to sleep inside, if that makes you uncomfortable. I'll sleep in my truck if I must, but I'm not leaving. Come on," he suggested softly. "Let's finish this discussion inside, where it's warm."

Back at the house; they removed their boots and slickers outside and joined Miller and Jack in the kitchen. Wade was a stranger; she shouldn't trust him. But she needed someone to depend on; and it discomfited her to know his good looks and fancy suit influenced her opinion. Grampa Morgan had always warned her to never judge a book by its cover. And here she was, doing just that. He'd be disappointed but she was running out of options. With few places left to turn, she'd accept his help, even if she was reluctant to do so.

"Are you letting him stay here?" Miller demanded of Jack. His tone left no doubt he was suspicious of Wade's motives.

"That's up to April," Jack replied. "She's the boss now."

"She doesn't have any legal right to the ranch, not until John is found or declared dead. And even then, known heir or not, there is no will." Miller's tone implied he didn't want April in charge.

"That don't matter none," Jack argued. "She *is* the rightful heir and I'll mind her orders."

"Wade is my friend, and he's staying for a while." The

words were out even before she realized she'd agreed to let a virtual stranger stay with her even though he could be dangerous and wasn't telling her everything. Heck, he hadn't told her anything about himself. But she felt safe alongside him. Safer inside this ranch house knowing that he was inside it too. Even after the debacle with her ex-husband, she trusted her instincts.

After a few minutes of uncomfortable small talk, Miller left. Even in the kitchen at the opposite end of the house, they heard mud spit from the tires of his RCMP issue SUV as he raced away.

CHAPTER SIX

"I'm not sure why you want to stay," April stated once Miller was gone.

"Me either," Jack agreed.

"I've got time on my hands; I haven't been on a ranch since I was a kid and I miss it. I'd love to have the full ranch experience. That should be reason enough. If it isn't sufficient, add in the fact that something isn't right here. I've got five-alarm safety warnings buzzing in my head. So, if you'll have me, I decided I'd hang around a while." Their suspicions of him were well placed. They didn't know who he was or why he was here. With things so muddled up on the ranch, they were right to be cautious.

"And eat up good food we ain't got money for?" Jack blurted.

"I'll be happy to pay my way. We could consider this…a dude ranch transaction. A business deal. I'll pay you a reasonable fee for the ranch experience." He liked the way the old cowboy stood up for April; his old-fashioned manners and gallantry were rare in the city; he was a relic from another time. Being here would give him plenty of opportunity to scout for land to buy for a place of his own, away from the hustle and bustle of the city.

"And what would you consider reasonable?" April asked.

"What do you provide to your bed and breakfast guests and what does it cost?" Wade didn't want to waste his money, but neither did he want to cheat them. Business dealings had taught him to ask leading questions to determine the boundaries and value of a contract.

April looked at Jack, questions in her eyes.

"You don't know?" Wade asked. "Don't you live here? Aren't you involved in the business?" Her lack of knowledge had him right back to wondering what her story was. According to Jack, she was heir to the ranch, but didn't seem to know much about how it worked. It probably tied into her being gone since her grandfather died, but it begged a dozen questions. Questions that would have to wait.

"I've only been here two months, and there haven't been any guests during this time." She flushed and looked away.

Wade was dumbfounded. How could you be in line to inherit a ranch and not know what the books looked like? Even if she'd arrived recently, she should have started learning the ropes before now. Her lack of business sense could be good for him, he could get steal of a deal if she was desperate for money. He winced mentally; it wasn't like him to consider taking advantage of someone less fortunate. He prided himself on his charity.

"What about the books? The accounting records?" Wade asked.

"You ask a lot of questions for a bystander," Jack accused.

"Relax, Jack," April patted him on the shoulder. "I don't

think Wade means us any harm. I think he's trying to help us out here. I'm reluctant to let a stranger in on my, on our, personal life, but frankly, I'm out of my element here. I'm a nurse, not a rancher. I've never tried to run a business, and I have no idea where to start. And I sure don't know anything about running a bed and breakfast. And I haven't been able to locate the books since I arrived. My uncle must have taken or hidden them."

Jack made a disgruntled noise and poured himself another coffee. "You folks want more?" When they declined, he returned the pot to the burner and switched the pot off.

"You need to locate those books."

"I've been looking in my spare time, and I've tracked my spending since I arrived. I know that's inadequate, but it'll do for now." Her hands twisted together until she flattened them on the table.

"I might be able to help. I know a bit about business," Wade offered the partial truth.

"I got that from the fancy suit you were wearing on your vacation," April teased.

Wade chuckled. "I've done some mentoring too. I'm on sabbatical, so what if we work out a deal, a contract if you will, for me to learn ranching while I teach you some business basics?"

"I'd like that," she concurred, glancing away, not meeting his gaze. "I ordered some business books online, but they haven't arrived yet. I'll make us a late lunch and after we get my truck running, we'll talk business." She offered her hand to Wade. "Deal?"

"Subject to a mutually acceptable price, I accept that deal," he agreed, shaking her hand briskly. Her small hand was soft and warm in his, tempting him to hold it longer than propriety demanded.

She sucked in a tiny startled breath, her gaze flying to his. She jerked her hand free of his and then pulled some roast beef and fresh vegetables from the fridge.

"What can I do to help?" Wade asked.

"Can you set the table? We'll have soup and sandwiches. It won't be fancy, but it'll fill us up and the soup will be warm." She stared out the window at the rain.

He debated asking about her pensive expression and decided against it. He barely knew her and had no right to pry into her thoughts, even if he was curious. She didn't seem all that reluctant to talk about the ranch; perhaps she'd open up about herself as well. He opened the cupboard she gestured to and pulled down some plates.

Lunch wasn't elaborate, but it was fresh and filling with enough substance to fuel a body and warm it all the way through. Hearty, homemade, vegetable-beef soup and thick roast beef and cheddar sandwiches with plenty of fresh lettuce and tomatoes from the garden.

"So how do we get the truck back here?" Wade asked. "Tow truck?"

"It's only a few miles. We can tow it back with the tractor. I'd like to get it back soon. There are groceries in the backseat. The perishables are in a cooler. I'd hate for them to go to waste. I should have brought them home with me, with us. Once the truck's back, Jack can try and figure out what's wrong with it. And if you don't mind, we can use yours to go to town for parts. I'll pay for the gas."

"That dilapidated heap is your only vehicle?" The rundown state of the ranch and the lack of vehicles, combined with Miller's unpleasant attitude, made Wade uncomfortable. What was the cop's issue? Something weird and unsettling was happening here. April and Jack both seemed like decent people, he was curious about what was really going on out here in the back of beyond.

"Unfortunately, it is. I ended up taking the bus here after my car died. We do have a couple old quads, but they aren't registered for use outside our property."

"I've tried to run a business without the proper equipment. It's not easy," he commiserated. "So, let's get that truck back here and get to work on it."

Side by side, they cleared the table and loaded the dishwasher. Jack thanked April for lunch and then headed out to do some chores before the rain renewed its assault.

"Do you have any work clothes?" April hung the dishcloth over the edge of the sink. "You can't work around here in those fancy duds."

Wade studied her. There was more to her question than she stated. He just couldn't understand what she was hinting at. "I've got some jeans. I'd rather not ruin them, and this could be a messy job." He left the statement open to interpretation.

"I'll get you some of Grampa Morgan's old clothes. I haven't gotten around to donating them to charity yet. They'll be too wide and too short, but they'll do for grubby work."

She left the kitchen. He heard her moving around down the hall and in minutes she was back in the kitchen. She handed him a pile of clean, worn clothing that included jeans, a faded 4H T-shirt and a sweater. Wade wrinkled his nose at the used clothing.

"What's the matter pretty boy? Never worn hand me downs before? Go ahead, they won't hurt you."

She was right, there was no harm in borrowing clothing to keep his from being damaged. He was being exactly the stuffed shirt type he despised. Had he grown that far out of touch with ordinary people? "Thank you. I'll change and we can get to work."

Inside the workshop, Wade climbed onto the tractor and tried unsuccessfully to start it. "How long has it been since you ran this thing?"

"Not since I've been here," she replied as he jumped down. "Any idea what the problem is?"

Wade checked the engine over and discovered several cut hoses and belts. He pointed them out to her. "Someone has gone to a lot of work to sabotage this engine. Fortunately, it looks fixable. Is there someplace close by where we can get parts?"

"The garage in town does triple duty. They do car repairs and sell equipment and parts and used cars. We'll be able to get what we need there. I'll rely on you to tell me what I need and I'll make a list. At least I have the tools. Grampa Morgan loved tinkering on vehicles. He has just about everything. I don't know anything about cars myself."

"I'm a half decent mechanic," Wade offered his services. "I've fixed up a lot of classic cars in my days. I haven't done much work on tractors, okay, I haven't done any," he chuckled. "But this is a classic and will likely be similar. An engine is an engine. I hope. If I run into issues, I'll just Google how to fix it. YouTube has everything." He rubbed his hands together enthusiastically and smiled at her.

The corners of her mouth turned down. "We don't have Internet. I had to cancel it because money's tight."

Dismay and anger marched up his spine. Why was this beautiful woman living like a pauper? The ranch seemed big enough and, from the looks of it, had once been prosperous. There were dozens of cows in the fields that could be sold for income. Had her uncle really done that much damage?

"Luckily, Internet is easily accessible by phone. Let's go get parts and get the truck home." He'd never been poor, but understood how corners had to be cut to save money; still, this was ridiculous.

Wilson's Garage was a nondescript building with faded blue and white paint. The multi-purpose business serviced a large rural area in terms of automotive repairs, farming equipment and parts for anything with a motor. There was even a small lot off to one side where they sold reconditioned cars. The parking lot was jammed with client vehicles waiting their turn for repairs in one of three service bays. The brick structure was three times as long as wide to accommodate the enormous parts department. A small, free-standing building was home to the car and tractor salesmen.

"What do you mean I can't put the parts on the ranch account?" April strained for calm. "The Lazy-W's had an account here for fifty years. We always pay our bills." At least she remembered her grandfather paying his bills when she visited as a child. She stared at Riley Wilson, owner of the garage in disbelief. As always, he was dirty and squinty-eyed.

"Sorry," Riley said, without an ounce of sympathy. "The

ranch already owes us too much. The bill's been outstanding since your grandfather died, and I can't risk adding more to it."

"Come on, Riley. You've known me since I was a kid. You used to come out to the ranch and play with me. Trust me. I'm going to get the ranch up and running and I'll pay you back every cent, with interest. I swear it. I swear on the Morgan name." She was getting tired of this crap. Half the town seemed to have it in for her. The ranch didn't have any credit left anywhere, not even the feed store. She'd hoped Riley would cut her a break.

"Honey, the Morgan name ain't worth shit around here anymore. There isn't a single person in this town, hell, in all of Yellowhead County that'll lend you a plugged nickel. You're on your own." He turned his back on her.

"Excuse me," Wade injected. "Do you have the parts?"

"What if I do? She ain't getting them on credit." Riley glanced dismissively at Wade, who had been hovering near the door waiting for April. "And you ain't getting them on credit either. I can tell by the looks of you that you're just as broke as she is."

April looked at Wade and grinned. He didn't miss the irony of the slur and his earlier reluctance to wear the used clothing. "I'll pay for them," Wade offered politely, frowning.

"Cash?" Riley demanded.

"No. With my platinum credit card." He produced the card and slapped it on the counter.

Riley snatched up the card and studied it closely. "You on the up and up?"

Wade nodded serenely.

"I'll have to call for verification to be sure."

"You do that," Wade suggested calmly. "Please get the parts so we can be on our way."

Riley slid the card into his pocket and headed for the parts room.

"I'll just hang onto my card while you're gone," Wade held out his hand.

"What are you suggesting?" Riley snarled, handing the card back.

"I'm not suggesting anything. However, if you can't be bothered to trust April, I can't be bothered to trust you. Turnabout is fair play." Wade smiled and Riley tossed him the credit card and stormed into the parts room.

April grabbed Wade's arm gently. "Wade, I can't let you pay for my parts. I'll figure this out another way. I won't take your money." She wouldn't accept his charity, no matter how badly she needed it. She'd sort this out on her own. She'd go to the bank for a loan against the land if she had to; if she could get a loan on land which she only sort-of owned. Despair churned in her stomach, and her lunch threatened to come back up.

Wade's warm hand covered hers, calming her frustration. "It's okay. We'll deduct the parts from my bill for my accommodation." He winked at her. "Besides, that jerk needed a lesson in manners and nothing commands respect like a platinum credit card."

"Really," April said, keeping her voice low. "I can't let you do this."

"And I won't let him disrespect you because of your uncle's issues. I'm not giving you the parts. I'm trading them for my vacation." There was a firm no-nonsense tone to his voice. It was the sound of a man used to getting his own way.

"If I didn't need these parts so badly, I'd tell him what he could do with them." She backed down on her refusal to accept help. "Man, I'd love to tell him where to stuff them. I've never seen a credit card like that one."

"That's because they don't hand them out to just anyone. Let it go. I've got this handled." Wade gave a nod toward the parts room and laughed loudly as Riley came out with a large box of parts. "Honey, are there any other parts places close by?" he asked April with a discrete wink.

"We could go into Edmonton. It isn't far."

"I have everything you need here," Riley groveled, clearly sensing he was going to lose a large sale to the distant competition.

"And when Miss Cooper returns for more parts?" Wade raised one eyebrow.

"I'll put them on her account," he agreed grudgingly as he tallied the parts and accepted Wade's card as payment.

"Oh, add the charges for towing to the bill, please. Miss Cooper's truck is stalled just outside of town. Fetch it home for us, will you?" Wade suggested.

April hid a smirk at Riley's cross expression and waited while he called Wade's bank to confirm the card was legitimate. He seemed stunned by what he was told by the person taking the call.

He gave Wade his receipt and smiled a fake smile. "If you need any other parts, just call and I'll deliver them immediately without a delivery charge. And I'll have one of the guys bring the truck back immediately." The words were the grudging acceptance of a man who had been put in his place.

"I'd appreciate it if you could tow it yourself. It's her only vehicle and I don't want to trust it to just anybody. She needs a safe ride until we get a chance to buy her a new one." Wade hinted that they might consider buying it from Riley before he dropped her keys on the counter.

"I'll do that Mr.—"

"Just Wade is fine. We're all friends here." He easily lifted the box and grinned at April. They left the shop with Riley sputtering at their backs.

"Let's get home and get that tractor running," Wade suggested.

April laughed. After a second, she sobered. "I shouldn't let you force him to bring the truck back. I can't afford it. I'll call and cancel."

"You'll do nothing of the sort," Wade chided gently. "That jerk needed to be taken down a peg or two. And I had the power to do it. So, I did. For you. You don't deserve that kind of disrespect. Nobody going through tough times needs to be shamed. He's arrogant and a bully. The only way to stop a bully is to out-bully him."

"What if he retaliates after you're gone?"

"He won't," Wade assured her.

"How can you know that?" He was hiding something from her; she could sense it. "What are you not telling me?"

Wade laughed. "The bank will have reassured him that there's no doubt I could pay that bill."

The statement didn't answer her question; there was more to this than he was letting on. Miller seemed to have hinted that Wade wasn't what he appeared to be. Fancy clothes, unusual credit card, Riley's sudden acceptance and Miller's recognition…it all added up to something. She just couldn't determine what. Who was Wade Kelly, really?

He'd admitted to having some business acumen and his stylish clothes reflected that. Maybe he was just what he seemed, a successful businessman. He could be a con man, but she doubted it. He seemed too honest and helpful for that. Still, she'd be on her guard while he was around. *Why the heck did he intimate we were a couple? What was the purpose of that?* It felt weird, in a good sort of way, to be linked romantically to him. She wouldn't mind having a strong, handsome man like Wade around all the time. Her heart skipped a beat and thundered ahead excitedly.

CHAPTER SEVEN

"You sure know your way around an engine." April sized up Mr. Moolah. How rich was he anyway? He didn't mind getting his fingers dirty and seemed to know what he was doing. Maybe he hadn't always had money. She watched those appendages twisting the nuts. She swallowed, shook her head. Stop it, April. You've been down this road before and you know better than to fall for a pretty face. She looked at the empty pasture to distract herself. Red was missing. She'd miss the old bull.

Progress on the tractor repairs was slow but steady. They were nearing the end. "So how do you know so much about motors?" she asked, unable to contain her curiosity.

"My foster father was a mechanic. I spent a lot of time working on vehicles with him. I started apprenticing right out of high school, intending to work at Ford, but I changed my mind and went into the oil patch. This tractor's not much different than any other vehicle. An engine's an engine. It's not really a big deal."

"Maybe not for you, but it is for me. I wouldn't know how to fix it. And Jack's busy on more critical chores. It could've been an eternity before this was looked at. I appreciate it. You've been my knight in shining armor all day. You've rescued me from one catastrophe after another. How do I thank you?" The words felt inadequate. She owed this handsome stranger so much and if he followed through on helping her with the business end of ranching, she'd owe him even more. A sigh slipped out.

She had to stop dwelling on the ranch's failings and focus on the positive. Like the bicep muscles bunching and flexing under Wade's shirt. A couple buttons on his western shirt had come undone. She stared at the gap, unable to tear her gaze away. Wade Kelly was one delicious hunk of manhood. Strong and caring, just what a ranch, and a woman needed. If she was looking for a man, which she wasn't.

"What is it, princess?" He rolled the mechanics creeper out from under the tractor and peered up at her. The creeper rolled smoothly on the concrete floor of the equipment shop. Grampa Morgan had always said that the money he put into the cement floor was worth every penny.

"You're not stressing over me helping, are you?

"A bit," she admitted, sliding her fingers through her hair. "I can't help it. I've never been beholden to anyone. I've always managed to make my own way. Well, until recently, that is. I have to confess; I'm struggling with my problems." She slapped a hand over her mouth. "Good grief, now I'm blurting out my issues to strangers."

"First off, a stranger is just a friend you haven't met, and after spending most of a day together, I'm starting to think of us as friends. Second, I'm paying for the privilege of living the ranch life. Fixing tractors is part of that. And third, working on cars is how I relax. From my perspective, this is working out okay. A win-win situation."

Wade tinkered and puttered with the tractor for close to an hour before he declared it fit for use. "It needs an oil change and more hydraulic fluid, but she'll work now."

"Thank you so much," April smiled warmly at him. The sound of an approaching vehicle interrupted her gratitude. A tow truck entered the lower yard. "I'll just pull the tractor outside. Can you get him to pull the truck inside for me?" She asked, climbing into the cab. Gracious, she hadn't been on the seat of this tractor since she was fourteen. Hopefully, she remembered how to control it. She drove the tractor through the elongated shop and out the equipment door on the other end without a hitch.

The neighbors had laughed at Grampa when he erected the oversized equipment shop, saying it was more than he'd ever use and a total waste of money. He'd proved them wrong again and again. Occasionally, when the weather was at its worst, Grampa had lent the space to neighbors, allowing them to do repairs out of the elements. The building was enormous. With three drive-through bays, each long enough for two pieces of farm equipment. There was a mezzanine level that had served as storage and a playroom for April on her summer visits to the ranch. More than one barn dance and barbeque had been held here. The shop nearly vibrated with positive memories.

Now, the shop was filled with discarded, broken-down equipment and junk. It needed a good cleaning. Some of the items would be sellable; even if it was just for scrap metal. Most of it was nothing more than garbage that should have been hauled away long ago. Grampa's biggest flaw had been his inability to part with anything that might prove useful later.

Climbing down from the tractor, she paused to watch Wade talk to Riley. Wade leaned against the tow truck, looking like something out of *GQ*. No man had the right to look that sexy in dirty, ill-fitting clothing. The sun had come out just enough to shine on his wavy, light brown hair. He looked good enough to eat.

Don't go there. Wade Kelly was a guest, a helping hand. He didn't belong on the Lazy-W, so there was no sense being attracted to him. Yeah, right. Too late on that one. The man was ridiculously attractive and well muscled, and, even under Grampa Morgan's overalls, she could imagine how nice it would be to touch his skin. He looked fit and strong and entirely too kissable.

April moaned aloud. It had been too long. Four months to be precise. Not since the night she accidentally conceived her baby with her jerk of an ex. She shouldn't have been talking to him, let alone sleeping with him. She'd been drinking when he showed up and she'd fallen, briefly, for his charm. Never again. Not with her ex, or any other man.

She couldn't hear what Wade said to Riley over the sound of the truck engine, but Riley's response made Wade laugh. The sound tickled across her skin and her heart rate jumped. Pushing the errant attraction aside, she strolled over to them. "Hi, Riley. Thanks for towing the truck home for me."

"Anything for you...and Wade."

And Wade, was right. The tone of Riley's voice left no doubt he'd done this for Wade, not her. Torn between gratitude and irritation, she forced a smile and asked him to pull the truck into the shop.

"Right-oh. Just like Wade told me to." He saluted, pulled in and dropped the broken-down truck off. With a wave, he left the yard.

Wade and April lugged the groceries up the hill to the house and put them away before returning to the truck. They were barely back when another truck pulled in and came to a stop near the bull paddock.

"Oh, that's Aki, the vet. You'll like her. She's friendly and beautiful." Crap, now it sounded like she wanted him to like the vet. Damn her errant mouth.

They hurried over to the white truck with AJM Vet Services printed on the doors. A tall thin woman with high cheek-bones and long shiny black hair climbed out of the truck.

"Hi, Aki. I'm not sure if you remember me. I'm April Cooper, Morgan's granddaughter." She offered her hand.

"Remember you? Heck yeah." She pulled April into a warm embrace. "We spent hours playing together when Dad came out here to look after the animals. Her warm smile faded minutely.

"How is your dad?" April asked, not sure she wanted to know.

"He passed last winter. I've taken over the business."

"Oh gosh, I'm sorry for your loss. Aki, this is my friend, Wade Kelly. Wade, this is Aki June-Moose. She's the vet and an old friend."

They shook hands. To April's eyes, it seemed like they held on just a touch too long. She shrugged the thought off.

What did she care if a man she hardly knew was attracted to Aki?

"Aki June-Moose? Is that Ojibwa?" Wade asked.

"It is. Nice catch. Most people assume Cree in these parts." June laughed, her deep brown eyes sparkling with attraction and she fluffed her hair.

Wade didn't seem to notice her flirtatious glance. "I've got an employee, with June-Moose as a last name. Best dang worker I've ever had."

"Anyway," April interrupted. "Red's over here." She waved toward the dead bull. "Sergeant Miller wants to know the cause of death. Not that there's any doubt."

"He mentioned that when he called. Seems like a ridiculous waste of my time to be here. But I go where I'm needed." She quickly braided her long black hair into a thick plait, slipped into some coveralls and boots and climbed over the fence, medical bag in hand.

April and Wade joined her alongside the bull.

"Well, no doubt here," she commented. "Dead center. Perfect. Right between the eyes. There isn't a chance in hell this was an accident. A shot that perfect took skill and intent. This bull was murdered."

"I'll extract the bullet and send it to the lab, along with some tissue samples, just in case something else is awry," Aki dug into her kit.

"Damn," April whispered softly.

Wade placed his hand on her shoulder.

The touch was comforting and a delicious little chill ran down her back. She could get used to being touched by Wade. His quiet strength bolstered her own. "I really hoped it was an accident."

"Well, aside from the obvious, why's that?" Aki carved carefully into the skull with a bone saw.

April grimaced and looked away, unable to see her animal friend being desecrated. "Crazy stuff is happening around here." April explained their situation. "I'm starting to think someone doesn't want me here."

"I agree. Listen, don't eat the meat from Red. I'm sure it's fine, even if it's been sitting for a couple hours. But with strange things happening, I'd just haul him into the far quarter and let the coyotes have him, or better yet, burn him, just in case someone tampered with his feed as well. And I'll keep my ears open. Occasionally I pick up a tidbit of information. People talk around me, sometimes, like I'm not even there. Dad always called it 'hired hand syndrome.'" She chuckled as she finished bagging her samples.

"Come up to the house for coffee," April offered as they climbed out of the enclosure.

"Gee, I'd love to, but I've got a couple calls to make this afternoon. I doubt I'll even make it home for supper. Ah, the life of a country vet. James Herriot had it so right, and so wrong. But, next time I'm out this way, I'll stop by, if that's okay?"

"Absolutely," April agreed, looking forward to renewing their friendship.

"So, how long are you staying?" Aki asked Wade boldly, while sexily wiggling out of her coveralls and boots.

April squinted at Aki jealously. The woman should just back off.

"Just here helping April out," he replied. "I'll stay as long as it takes, then I have to get back to business."

"And what, exactly, is business?" Aki asked, reaching out to brush her hand on his shoulder.

April fumed, jealousy getting her hackles up.

"Oh, this and that," Wade evaded, slinging his arm casually over April's shoulders.

Aki glanced from one to the other, questions in her eyes. April gave a half-smile. Whatever Wade's reason for his action, April liked that he didn't seem attracted to her beautiful friend and that he had no compunction about letting her know. She shouldn't be pleased about it, she shouldn't even care as she hardly knew the man, but that small semi-embrace felt good.

"Thanks for coming, Aki. Please send me the bill."

"No worries. The RCMP called me. They'll get the bill for this one." She grinned. "Besides, Miller's been riding everyone's ass since his son went AWOL. He's got a bee in his bonnet for sure. Time to return the favor. He can pay it. You've got enough on your plate right now. Take care. See you around." She gave Wade one last inviting smile and climbed into her truck.

"What's next, boss lady?" Wade asked.

They still stood side by side, his arm slung over her shoulders. April took a deep breath, inhaling his masculine scent. He smelled like hard work, man and sex appeal. She inched away; she was enjoying the feel of his arm way more than she should.

"I wonder what she meant by Miller's son going AWOL?" She shrugged, dislodging his arm. "I guess we better haul Red out into the field and burn him," she whispered, hating the sadness in her voice. "Then I'll need to cook supper and we can get down to learning the business of business."

Wade chuckled. "Okay, let's get this done. Tomorrow, we can get started on truck repairs. I hope we need parts so I can make Riley bring them out."

"Gosh, I don't. I can't afford any more expenses. There's not a penny in the ranch accounts, not that I have access to them anyway. Uncle John disappearing has been a big pain in the backside. Don't get me wrong, I'm glad I had the ranch to come home to when my life turned to crap, but everything's just a huge mess right now."

"Why did your life turn to crap?" he asked.

"Because my ex-husband is a jerk. But, we're divorced, so it's all good from here on out." Her marriage was long since finished. She didn't even want to think about her stupidity in sleeping with him and ending up pregnant.

Wade paused mid-step. "I think there's more to it than that."

"Yup. But this is personal. Come on Wade, you're hardly more than a stranger. I'm not dumping my problems on you. You've done so much for me already. Let's just get this cremation over with and move on." She hadn't even known him for a day, and she was utterly dependent on him and wanted to unburden herself to him. Nope. She was stronger than that. Besides, he was a successful business man and she was an out of work nurse and destitute rancher. He was way too good for her, even if he was damned cute. Besides, he reeked of money and there was no way she'd fit into a world like that. She was a simple woman with simple tastes and strong enough to stand up alone.

Wade's gaze skipped over her face as he studied her. April could tell he wasn't happy with her evasion, but as much as she needed his help, she wasn't going to jeopardize it by letting him know she'd been accused of theft and fired from her last job. No charges had been filed, but you never knew what her jackass ex might do next; she was certain he'd been behind her firing. She remained silent, avoiding Wade's questioning gaze.

Eventually, Wade seemed to accept her desire to bury the past and nodded his agreement to let it go.

CHAPTER EIGHT

After a supper of leftover roast beef, mashed potatoes and fresh salad, Jack went to supervise the cremation fire. They'd piled up some old wood and used the tractor to drop the bull on top. The wood would act as a fire base. Jack would add more as the fire burned lower. He'd keep at it until the entire bull was gone. They'd bury the bones later. April and Wade sat at the desk in the office, compiling bank statements and the limited financial records they could locate.

Wade stared in dismay around him. Papers were piled willy-nilly around the office; they covered the chairs and the desk and spilled haphazardly out of the filing cabinet. It would take forever to find anything in this mess. A soft groan of dismay escaped him, causing April to turn and grimace at him.

"I know, it's terrible. I've been working on it, but it feels like I'm not getting anywhere. But there are only so many hours in a day, and actual ranching takes up a lot of time. I've made a pile of bank statements, but some are missing. They're probably here someplace." She gestured helplessly around the office. "At least I hope they are."

She explained her somewhat unorthodox sorting system to him and they started to work, hoping to determine what caused the ranch's financial crisis, as well as set up a proper bookkeeping system.

They located bank statements up to the point where Uncle John had taken over running the ranch. After that there was a huge and very telling gap of records until he disappeared. After that point, they had the past year's statements and records of all the money Jack and April had spent since she arrived. The account was well in arrears. It was a wonder the bank hadn't closed it out long before now.

"I assumed a ranch this size would have computerized records. Don't ranchers keep detailed accounts of the stock bloodlines? I don't know much about cattle, but wouldn't breeding records be important?" Wade questioned her.

"There used to be an ancient computer. I haven't seen it since I arrived. But then, I haven't had time to look for it, either. I'm using the shoebox method of accounting," she chuckled.

"Tell me you're kidding." He stared at her, unable to overcome his shock and dismay that anyone running a business would use shoebox accounting.

"I told you, I don't know anything about accounting. I can balance a check book and know how to save for retirement and run a monthly budget. But full-out bookkeeping is beyond me. That's why I used the last of the space on my credit card to order accounting books. Animal husbandry books I've got in droves."

"You need to start recording everything." He hadn't been

expecting her to need the basics. This could take ages. He wasn't sure he was prepared to put in that much time, but how could he leave her in the lurch?

"I'm not that stupid," she declared with a laugh. "I'm writing everything down and saving the receipts...in a shoebox. I'm even keeping a running total." She stuck her tongue out at him. "So there, not as dumb as you thought I was," she teased.

Good Lord. She was acting like a three-year-old and all he wanted to do was kiss the sass right out of her. He'd only known her for a day and already he was feeling off-balance. He couldn't even remember the last time he felt an uncontrollable urge to kiss a woman. Damn! He'd made a mistake staying here. A big mistake. If he fell for her, even a little, there was no way he'd want to buy her out of her family home. He didn't have principles like that.

"Show me this alleged accounting system," he ordered teasingly.

"Stay here." She held up a hand in a stop motion. "I'll go get it."

"You don't keep it in the office?"

"Nope." She hurried out of the room.

He listened to her steps as she raced up the stairs. Something heavy shifted overhead, a door slammed and the shifting sounded again. She thundered back down the stairs and reappeared, slightly dusty, in the office.

"You hide the books?" She was nuts, she had to be, why else would she hide the books?

April blushed. "Um. Yeah."

"Care to explain?" he asked as she set the box on the desk between them.

"You have to ask?" She quirked one eyebrow at him. "Strange crap is going on here. Stuff is missing. The ranch records are gone. Bank statements have vanished and I've lost two pieces of jewelry since I arrived. And I know Jack didn't take them. They weren't even valuable, just simple gold chains and pendants. I just know they disappeared. I did not lose them. So, a good defense is the best offense."

"That makes sense," he agreed.

She was smart to hide valuables if things on the Lazy-W were as crazy as she claimed. Now if only they knew where the computer had vanished to.

"Jack says the computer disappeared right after Grampa got sick. So, it's likely Uncle John got rid of it."

"Maybe. Would your grandfather have been well enough to hide it?" An idea was gelling in his mind. An ugly idea.

"Maybe. Why?"

He could tell the idea appealed to her even if it didn't make sense. "I'm thinking that if your grandfather believed your uncle was up to no-good, he might have hidden it. Is there any place he stored valuables that your uncle might not know of?"

"No. I don't think so—" Her eyes widened and she leapt up from the chair she'd just settled in. "Maybe." She raced out of the room.

Wade followed, hot on her heels, across the hall into the master bedroom.

"Give me a hand with this!" she demanded, trying to shift the extra-thick, oversized-mattress. Together they heaved it off the bed, covers and all, and leaned it against the wall.

"Shoot," she declared, hands on her hips, staring at the

wooden bed platform. "I'll need a Number Eight Robertson screwdriver."

"You know what a Robertson is? Most people call it a square head." This woman had facets he hadn't imagined.

"I'm a nurse, not an idiot. Hang on. There's one in the kitchen." She was back in seconds, brandishing the screwdriver triumphantly.

"You think a sick old man took apart his bed and hid a computer? That's insane." The woman was losing her marbles. Red's death must have put her over the edge.

"No, but he did have a nurse for a couple months. She could have done it for him." She worked frantically at the myriad of screws securing the flat top that served as a box-spring. She reached across the bed to hand him the screws as she worked. "I remember when Grampa Morgan built this bed. It was my idea to have a secret space. I was a kid, and I loved hidey-holes."

"Couldn't we just take out the drawers," he asked, studying the multi-drawer unit.

"Nope. There's a secret space near the top, it would be tight for a computer, but it might fit..." She trailed off on a grunt, prying the wood up and trying to slide it lower.

Wade dropped the screws into a decorative blue and white bowl on the dresser and helped her shift the platform.

"Yes," she cried ecstatically, reaching in and extracting a laptop. "Wow, this must be old, it's huge. It barely fit in the hole. Grab that cord, will you?" She thrust her chin toward the opening.

Wade reached in and tugged on the cord. It caught on something else and he shifted the platform wood lower. Do you want this other stuff too?" He asked.

"There's more?"

"A couple small things," he grunted, reaching lower to grab them. "It's a velvet bag and a small box" He straightened and handed them to her.

"She stroked the polished wood box, tracing the grain lines with her fingertips after blowing off a thick layer of dust. "Is that everything?" She peered under the bed herself.

"Looks like it. Let's get the bed back together and fire that baby up." He eased the board back in place, grabbed the screwdriver she'd dropped and then began replacing the screws. A soft whisper of sound made him pause and look at her.

She sat on the floor, curled up tight, tears streaming down her face.

What the hell? Why wasn't she celebrating? They'd found the computer and could hit the books hard. Three long strides carried him around the bed. He settled beside her on the floor, drawing her into his embrace. He didn't know the cause of her distress but suspected that whatever was in that small box was at fault. He stroked her back and murmured comforting words. Slowly, her sobs eased. He handed her a tissue from the nightstand and she blew her nose loudly and wiped her face.

"Sorry," she whispered. "I didn't mean to fall to pieces."

"It's been a long rough day for you. You're entitled to a bit of weeping."

"I don't cry," she sniffed loudly.

He chuckled. "Nice try, princess. It's okay to cry."

Good gravy, he wanted to know what had brought on the tears, but he was still a stranger and, for now, he'd be content to comfort her without knowing what had caused the dam to break. He paused, mid-thought. He hated weepy women. They made him crazy-uncomfortable. So why didn't April's tears bother him? They did bother him, but he wanted to help. He didn't have his usual "oh my God, get me out of here" response.

"I'm fine, now." She eased out of his embrace and stood. "Let's get this bed back together and fire up that laptop. When did Grampa get a laptop?" she mused aloud. "He had an ancient desktop last time I was here? Of course, that was years ago, just before Uncle John showed up. I mean, I was back for the funeral, but computers weren't exactly on my priority list."

Wade chuckled, and she froze in the process of re-sheeting the bed to stare at him.

"What?" she demanded.

"You're babbling again."

"No, I'm not. I don't babble. Sure, I sometimes talk too much. But I don't babble. I don't know why you'd even say that. You hardly know me."

His laugh interrupted the torrent of words and she blushed a delightful pink.

"Okay. Maybe I do. A little."

She kept quiet while they finished making the bed, though he could see the effort it took. He was learning she babbled to work things out in her head and he was certain that most of the time she didn't even know she was doing it. The habit was adorable and endearing.

CHAPTER NINE

Ten minutes later, they sat across from each other at the kitchen table. The velvet bag, the wooden box and the computer between them. April plugged in the laptop to charge and sat stroking the newly dusted box.

"Tell me about the box," Wade requested.

April looked at him and puffed out a breath. This was going to be hard. So many memories, so many emotions. "Grampa Morgan made this." She stroked it again. It was glass-smooth under her fingertips. "He made it for Grammy. For their anniversary. He took almost a full year to carve it and fit the pieces together." She traced the interlocking swirl inlays. "He worked in secret. I remember when he gave it to her. I must have been eight. Maybe."

April swallowed a baseball of emotion before it choked her.

"Grammy cried and cried. She was so happy. When I asked why she cried or if she was happy, she said she had everything she had ever wanted. That he'd given her everything she asked for, everything money could buy. But the box was special. He'd taken the time, so many hours to make it. Just for her. I thought she was silly. Now, I see how much love went into this small box and how the work was a declaration of his love for her." Tears overwhelmed April, and she buried her head in her arms, struggling to battle the pain and the joy of rediscovering the precious trinket.

"Wow," Wade said quietly. "He must have really loved her."

"He did."

"Is there anything inside it?"

"Just this old key. I've never seen one like this before. It's weird." She held up the key for his inspection, keeping it just out of his reach. She couldn't bear to have him touch it yet. Somehow it felt like it should be important. Why else would Grampa Morgan hide it?

"That's old. I've never seen one like it. Maybe we can search the Internet later on my phone and see what it might have opened. It must have been important to your grandfather if he went to the trouble to hide it."

April got up and rummaged through a drawer. She returned to the table with a long string of leather cording. She looped it through the key and hung it on her neck, tucking it inside her shirt, next to her heart. Thankfully, Wade didn't comment on her actions. It'd be hard to explain her thinking, not that she'd really thought the action through. Protecting the key was…instinctive rather than reasoned out.

They sat quietly, drinking their tea for a while before she mustered the courage to pick up the blue velvet drawstring bag. It wasn't large. Only about ten centimeters square. It was dusty and faded and strangely felt precious. She couldn't shake the idea she was holding a piece of history.

She opened it and carefully poured the contents into her hand. Granny's diamond wedding set sat in her palm, the three rings glittering at April. Beside it lay an unfamiliar emerald ring and a crudely made bracelet of poorly polished stones.

Tears welled in her eyes.

"Oh. My. I made this," she whispered and stroked each of the stones in turn. "I couldn't have been more than ten or eleven. I had a rock tumbler. I polished the stones and glued caps on the ends to string them together. And they kept it. I thought it was long gone. It's just a piece of junk and they kept it." Tears rolled unchecked down her cheeks and she didn't even care. All that mattered was this lasting testimony to her grandparents' love for her and for each other.

"You should find a safe place to keep these rings," Wade advised.

"You don't think I should sell them?" she asked, bewildered.

"They're part of your heritage. I wouldn't sell them except as a last resort. History is important."

"I'm at my last resort," she sighed. "I guess they have to go." It would break her heart to sell them, but the money could really help the ranch. Maybe not enough to get back on its feet, but enough to pay some bills.

"Not yet, you aren't. We can figure out the books and see if we can plan this ranch back into success. If that doesn't work, we'll try something else. And something else after that. There has to be a way for you to keep the ranch and the rings."

"Why?" One simple word, straight from her aching heart

and it implied so many questions. Questions she couldn't even formulate, let alone ask a stranger.

"Because family and heritage are important. I lost my family when I was six. All I have left is my mother's wedding ring and a couple of faded pictures. I have my foster parents, but not my birth parents. I know about family and loss. And dammit, I'm going to help you keep yours."

How dreadful to lose your family like that. She'd been an adult when Grampa Morgan and her father died. Now she was alone, except for Uncle John, and he was missing and he'd run the ranch into the ground. But to lose them as a child? Terrible. Unthinkable.

"I'll hide them away. We need to get back to the books," she declared, surging to her feet enthusiastically. "I need to save the Lazy-W." She picked up her tea and the laptop and headed for the office.

She had the laptop plugged back in and turned on before he joined her. When it finally finished booting up, she opened a file.

"Look," she exclaimed, staring at the screen. "All the birth records until 2009, that's when Grampa started to get sick. Uncle John was here then."

She scrolled around a bit. "And here's the accounting program. Woohoo!"

"That's excellent. Now we just need to piece in the missing years. How many? Six?"

"Between six and seven," she sighed. "That's a lot of missing paperwork."

"I don't want to add to the burden, but you need to contact Revenue Canada to find out the last year taxes were filed."

"Shit." She slapped a hand over her mouth. "I mean darn." Her head dropped dramatically against the back of the chair. "I don't even want to know." Just what she needed, an enormous bill for back taxes and interest. Not.

"I don't blame you." He came around the desk and laid a comforting hand on her shoulder. "But I do know they'll go easier on you if you're up front about trying to straighten things out. And, you'll want to contact everyone who might be owed money and let them know you're working on a repayment plan…before someone slaps a lien on the ranch."

"Holy crap. I hadn't even thought about that. I'm not cut out for this."

"Maybe not, but I can teach you a lot and help you deal with things," Wade offered.

"Why?" She demanded, suspicious of his motives. "Why are you taking such an interest in my affairs? I appreciate the effort, but I'm wondering… are you just kind, or do you have an ulterior motive?" His insistence on helping perplexed her. Kindness of strangers was one thing; this was above and beyond. It touched her, and it worried her, right down to her toes.

"Don't be cynical, April. You need help and I was raised to help out when needed. I don't know anything about ranching, but I do know business."

He looked so earnest and straight-forward that she believed him. Almost. He was so handsome and so helpful, and yet strangely evasive about his business.

"What business?" she demanded. Could he have an ulterior motive for being here? Maybe he'd known who she was when he stopped to assist her. Maybe, he knew the ranch was in trouble and wanted to buy it out from under her.

Chills wracked her; she clenched her fists. No, she wouldn't think that of him, he was just a good man, trying to help.

"I own an oil-field service company. I've left it in the hands of my second-in-command while I take some time off. He's not expecting me to be back for a couple weeks. Therefore," he said formally, "I can afford to give you a few days of my time. I can relax and do a bit of riding, help with chores and teach you accounting. I'll be killing two birds with one stone."

"More like six or seven," She studied him closely for signs of deceit. After the crap her ex had put her through, she'd learned a lot about the subtle signs of dishonestly. Shifty eyes, restlessness, unwarranted tension. There had to be a dozen signs. And he wasn't showing any of them. Well, except for not mentioning the name of his business, making her wonder what other secrets he had. If only she had Internet…

"I suggest we start a new accounting file with what records we have and go from there."

With that, they settled in. Wade stood behind her, offering help when she needed it, until she got a handle on the program. It was well after midnight when she declared herself competent, with the use of the help files, to go it alone.

She shut down the program and stood, stretching and twisting to relieve the kinks in her back. She about jumped out of her skin when Wade started to massage her shoulders. She jerked out of his reach.

"Please don't." She whirled around to scowl at him.

"I was just—"

"I don't know you well enough for that kind of behavior. Please keep your hands to yourself." She was overreacting but couldn't stop herself. She hadn't minded him comforting her earlier. But this, this bothered her for some reason. Maybe he was moving too fast, either that or she was totally misreading his intentions. Between the upheaval at the ranch and her pregnancy hormones, she was twitchy and emotional.

Wade held up his hands in an "I surrender gesture" and backed away. "Sorry, I didn't mean to upset you. It won't happen again."

Now why does that statement disappoint me? Maybe because she was inordinately attracted to him. He was handsome, helpful and sexy as sin, even in her grandfather's old clothes. But it was more likely his hands just felt too darned good, as if he'd sensed exactly what she needed.

"Thank you for respecting my wishes," she said formally.

His lip quirked in a wry half-grin. "Anytime."

"I think it's way past bedtime. Morning comes early on a ranch." She waved toward the door. "You can sleep in the spare bedroom. I'll sleep upstairs."

After saying good night, they went to their separate rooms. She waited almost an hour before sneaking downstairs for the shotgun she kept hanging high on the wall behind the kitchen door. She might not be alone, but she wasn't an idiot.

CHAPTER TEN

Overnight, a downpour pounded the house, the comforting sound of rain on the tin roof lulling her to sleep. When the sun came up, the rain faded to a misty drizzle. The world beyond her window looked fresh and new in the sun where it peeked out from between the clouds; but before long, the clouds drifted closer until the ranch was blanketed under a thick layer of dismal gray. Gloom hung heavy over the trio huddled at the kitchen table. April had slept deeply but woke feeling uneasy.

"After that storm, I have to check fences today," April stated between mouthfuls of blueberry pancakes.

"Won't it wait?" Wade asked.

"I have to check for trees down and fallen wires. Storms wreak havoc with fences and I can't afford to lose any more cattle."

"More cattle?"

"You heard Miller; someone's been rustling cattle in the area. Several cows from other ranches ended up on our land, but two-dozen of ours have gone missing. We won't be sure until fall, but we have a pretty good idea of how many should be in each field."

"Are you taking Jack with you?"

"There's a leak in the barn roof that needs to be repaired," Jack stated between bites. "And someone has to watch that bred heifer. I thought she'd drop last night, but that calf'll come soon. But I'll go if you want to deliver that calf." He smirked at Wade.

April chuckled. "You know darn well that she'll deliver without help."

"True enough, but I like to keep close, just in case."

Caution made sense to Wade, ranchers kept a close eye on their birthing stock. "I know absolutely nothing about delivering a calf. But I've been on a horse before." It wasn't a lie, exactly. He'd been on a horse when he was a kid. Three or four times. How hard could it be? It was like riding a bike, wasn't it?

"Good, then you go with April and I'll keep an eye on things here," Jack decreed.

"Don't you have quads? Don't ranchers use quads these days?"

"We have a couple, but I'm heading into the valley and I'd rather not walk all the way lugging a chainsaw. Quads won't safely cross the rockiest places. Horse's will get us closer. We'll bring a pack-horse with some wire and a couple of temporary metal posts. They're lighter and faster to use than driving new wooden ones." She rose and put her dishes in the sink.

"You wearing that?" Jack asked Wade with a chuckle.

Wade looked at his legs. "Are there more dry pants? Yesterday's are still damp and these dress pants won't cut it."

"I'll find you more. You won't need much. You won't be here long, anyway."

"I'll be here as long as it takes," he quipped, only to be interrupted by the ringing of his cell phone. He pulled it out of his pocket and Jack and April left the room.

~

"WADE SPEAKING."

"Wade is it now? What happened to Borne?" His best friend and business associate, Bronson Randolph, laughed. "Hiding your identity again?"

"I am. What do you need and this better be life or death?" Wade warned lightly. He was officially on sabbatical, no unnecessary calls; even though he was searching for property.

"We've got some issues with the Sunrise Energy contract. You need to look at it."

"That's why we have a legal department. Ten lawyers should be able to handle a simple contract." Frustration rocked him. He loved his business, but days like today, when nobody could make a simple decision, were what caused him to walk away, if only temporarily.

"They want your input."

"I put you in charge, Bronson. Handle it. Unless someone dies or blows up a rig, I don't care. I'm on sabbatical until I decide…"

"Decide what? That you're being a baby and running away?"

"I'm sick of the stress and the hectic second-to-second pace. I can't handle it. My heart's going to explode if I don't take a break. I need to get away from the stress, the people, but most of all the dinners with damned lying, cheating, and crooked politicians. WKB Well Servicing is my life, but it's killing me. Make the damned decision. It's your job."

"This needs your touch," Bronson pleaded.

"Bronson, handle it. Do what you think I'd do. I've been training you for years. I have every confidence you can manage this. And if you screw up, we'll take the hit, no blame on you."

"The shareholders?"

"The shareholders can kiss my ass," Wade growled.

"Okay," Branson hesitated. "If you say so, but I'm not sure I'm the man for the job."

"Bronson, you are the man for the job, or I wouldn't have left you in charge. And I'll send you an e-mail tonight. There's something I need you to have the lawyers investigate. Don't forget you're in charge." They exchanged a few pleasantries and disconnected just as April came back into the kitchen.

"In charge of what?" she asked.

"My company. I'm on sabbatical and I left Bronson at the helm." It was an answer, and the truth, but not the entire truth. Hopefully enough to satisfy but not lead to more questions.

"Okay." She shrugged as if she'd been expecting a more complete answer and was disappointed not to get it. "Anyway, here are a few of Grampa Morgan's clothes. I thought Jack would want you to move to the bunkhouse, but he insists I don't sleep in the house alone. Although, I don't see why a virtual stranger is better than alone." She sighed.

"I'd call it a judgment call. Some people are good at reading others. Maybe Jack's like that?"

"Funny you'd take his side," she quipped ironically. "But I

guess you might be right. I know I don't have that gift." She thrust the clothing into his arms. "Get changed and grab a slicker and rubber boots. It's going to be wet out there. I'll meet you down by the barn."

He made quick work of changing into the well-worn but clean clothing. April was right, the clothing fit poorly. Like yesterday, everything was too wide and too short. Her grandfather must have been short and stocky. When Wade pulled his socks up, he was just able to tuck the jean legs into them. That'd keep the bugs out, at least. And too short was better than too tight. He hesitated at the last second and slipped his wallet and keys under the mattress for safe keeping. He wouldn't need them to fix fences and he wasn't ready to reveal his full identity.

The barn, once a grand dame, had fallen into disrepair. Jack's story of the slow decline explained that. The boy inside the man begged Wade to pitch in and restore the ranch to its former glory. His inner businessman warned him that ranching was a tough haul and not the kind of life he was accustomed to, so he shoved the idea aside, hoping it wouldn't fester and nag at him.

This place was a crap-storm of problems and unresolved issues. It didn't make sense that someone would shoot the bull or rustle the cows. One push on that barn, and it would all be over. It didn't add up, but he'd assist for a while and move on with no regard for the attractive woman running things. Besides, if he stuck around, he might learn more; like if they were going to have to sell. This area of land was beautiful. He needed to google the land title map for this area and see just how much acreage this ranch covered.

April was waiting for him when he got to the barn. High

astride her horse, she was beautiful. The low light under the morning clouds didn't dim the sparkle in her brown eyes. Sitting there, she radiated comfort and competence. Her shining, freshly washed, hair drew him like a magnet. God, he could almost feel his fingers in those long strands. Smooth, silky and sexy. He shook the thought away. She held the reins to the other two horses. One with a saddle for Wade, the other carried a pack with tools sticking out over the top of it.

"Mount up, city-boy."

He recognized the taunt for the test that it was. Recalling his childhood lessons, he braced himself and slid his left foot into the stirrup and, with a light hop, swung his right leg over and settled into the saddle on the tan horse.

"You should have checked the cinch strap to be sure it was tight before you mounted," she chided gently.

"So, I failed your test then?" He winked.

"I'll give you a conditional pass since you didn't land on your backside. That's Mustard. He's an old hand with greenhorns. This is Pepper." She patted the mottled black and white horse she sat on.

"Mustard and Pepper? You named your horses after condiments?" He chuckled.

"Salty Dog is in the corral along with Garlic and Chives. Charlie Chaplin is hauling our gear. Those two scoundrels are Sage and Dalton. They're Australian Shepherds, cattle dogs. You met Biscuit already. She's older and probably napping on the porch."

"They're coming? Isn't it too wet for them?" Poor dogs would freeze to death.

"Sage and Dalton aren't your citified dogs. They're working animals. They live outside and earn their keep.

They're used to rain and snow. And they're the best damned cattle dogs this side of Edmonton. They can round up a herd without a single command. That's handy if there's a break in the fence."

"If you say so…" He settled himself in for the ride. Ready, he gave April another glance. It occurred to him she could sell a couple of horses for income, but what, exactly, was a horse worth these days? He tabled the idea for later consideration. He was going to need his full faculties about him if this turned into a long ride.

"Is that a rifle?" He waved at what appeared to be the stock of a gun sticking out from a scabbard near the pommel of her saddle.

"Grampa Morgan's old British 303. Got a problem with that?" She squinted at him and urged the horse forward slowly.

He hastened to catch up, thankful for those vacation riding lessons as a kid. "You know how to use it?"

"Damned right. Do you?"

He hesitated, before confessing his ineptness. "Not exactly. I've shot a gun before, but I'm pretty much new to firearms. So, I'll trust you to use it."

She laughed. "Indeed. Remind me to give you a few lessons. If you're going to live on a ranch, you need to know how to handle a gun properly and shoot what you're aiming at."

Live on a ranch? Why wasn't the idea repelling? It had a strange appeal, especially when he thought about living on this ranch, with this woman. He glanced at her from the corner of his eye. Her wheat blonde hair was caught up in a long braid that glistened in the dim light. She sat tall and confident in her saddle. A half-smile graced her lips and he wanted to taste that smile. He resisted the urge. His presence on the Lazy-W was temporary at best, and he certainly wasn't looking for a relationship; especially not one with a woman who needed money to bolster her floundering ranch. He'd had enough of gold-diggers.

The thought froze him in place. She didn't seem like a gold-digger. She seemed content, but worried about things. She'd tried to refuse his money all along, even going so far as to make him sign loan papers for the money he'd spent on tractor parts, despite their partial agreement for him to be a paying, working ranch hand. She wasn't hiding her problems, but she wasn't asking for help, financial or otherwise. He admired her pride and determination.

They rode in silence through the yard, past the house and guest cabins and down a narrow trail. She taught him the basic rule of gates. If you opened it, you closed it. And informed him that on the Lazy-W, gates were always closed, so if one was left open, something was amiss. They travelled for a long while, and Wade bumped uncomfortably along behind her.

"Relax," she chided. "It's only worse if you fight it. Move with the horse. Stop trying to stay rigid. I'm not going to regret bringing you along, am I?"

"No, ma'am," he grunted through gritted teeth. "I'll figure this out." He did his best to follow her instructions and finally managed to achieve something that resembled a comfortable position. This was going to be a long day, and he'd ache like hell by the end of it.

"So why the gun?" he asked at last, curiosity overcoming him.

"Aside from the fact someone shot one of my bulls in the head? Cougars, coyotes, bears, wolves…Ranching isn't an easy life. You have to be prepared to protect yourself. We've had crazy weather this year. Animal feeding patterns are off. We lost a barn cat last week to what we expect was a hungry coyote. I don't plan on feeding them again."

"And you're comfortable taking an animal's life for something besides food?" he asked. He understood the necessity of protecting your livestock, but the idea still didn't sit well.

"If, and only if, I must. All life is sacred. Warning shots often work, but I'll shoot something if there's no other option. It would be naïve to think there was another way."

They reached a fence line and followed the barbed-wire strands uphill for several minutes before she stopped and dismounted. The dogs raced ahead and back, tails wagging, noses sniffing for anything of interest.

"Don't bother getting down." She made quick work of attaching a loose fence strand before remounting.

"That was fast," he complimented her.

"Some repairs are easier than others. Plus, there's no time to waste. More weather coming in and we've got a ways to go."

"Um, how far exactly?" He was rethinking his decision to tag along.

"I'd planned on riding the perimeter of the sections we own. I'll do the leased quarters tomorrow. So, six miles total."

"How long does that take?" Crap in a hand-basket. Maybe he should have been more forthcoming about his lack of riding skills; but on the up-side, he knew how much land she owned, without goggling land maps.

"Depends on if the weather holds, how much damage there is, if any trees have fallen…a lot of factors. But you can count on two hours riding, total. More or less."

"Without a break?"

She laughed. "The only break you'll get is climbing down to drive in posts or nail up wire. Is that a problem, city-boy?" she teased lightly, a chuckle in her voice.

"Um. Nope. No ma'am, princess. I'll be fine," he lied.

"You'll be so sore you'll wish you'd never met me. Fess up, when's the last time you were on a horse?" She pivoted to stare at him.

Heat rose in his cheeks. "I might have misled you a bit." Damn, she'd caught him out.

"A lot?"

"Okay, a lot. I took riding lessons in Saskatchewan when I was fourteen. Rode every day for a week. I've only been on horseback maybe…twice since then." He winced at the confession and the pain in his backside.

"That's what I figured. Lucky for you, Jack's bringing the quad to meet us on the other side of this ridge, so another twenty minutes or so. We'll still be working, but you'll be off the horse."

"Another test?" he asked lightly, wondering if she'd ever trust him. But then, why would she? He'd kept information from her and she'd caught him in a lie more than once.

"Another test. You failed this one by the way. You should've been honest. I can't abide a liar."

The terrain was rough. Large boulders and rocks were strewn through the tree line. They wove in and out of the trees as they rode. It was old-growth forest and the spruces were enormous. In places they barely got the horses through. Now he understood why they hadn't taken a vehicle. They rode in silence for a few minutes, enjoying the fresh air and the scent of pine released when the horses brushed the trees.

"April?" he queried.

"Yes?" She slowed her horse to ride alongside him.

"I apologize for being dishonest." He continued after a brief pause. "I haven't told you everything about me. I can't get into my life story, yet. I just want you to know there are things I haven't told you."

"I'm aware of that." She studied his face as they rode. "Want to tell me why?"

"Okay," he said slowly. "I don't know you well and I tend to be a private person. I don't like my life being subject to public scrutiny." And a dozen other reasons he wasn't mentioning. His stomach clenched at the continued deceit. He was walking a narrow line here and it disturbed his equilibrium.

"So, you're willing to help with my ranch by paying to stay, and I should accept that without knowing who you are?" Her tone landed squarely between confusion and pique.

"When you put it that way, it is unfair of me. Can I have time to think before I explain?" It occurred to him she should refuse his request. She certainly had every right to and every right to turf him off her land. In her position, Wade wouldn't trust a stranger.

"Time to choose what to reveal, or what lie to tell me?"

"Ouch. I suppose I deserved that." Somewhere, in her past, there must be someone who had lied to her. Why else would she be so wary? He knew about deceit and losing your trust in others. "I don't suppose it would be enough to promise I won't lie to you? Omit details, yes. But I won't outright lie."

When she didn't respond, he made a confession. "I've been lied to on more than one occasion. I'm not talking little white lies, like being decades off a horse, but big lies. Ruin your plans and your life type lies. I promise I'll never lie to you like that."

"Who lied to you? Who ruined your life?" She pushed, hopping down from her horse and gesturing for him to do the same. "I'll hold this post. You use that post driver to pound it in." In between blows, she repeated the question. "Who hurt you?"

"Who hurt you?" he countered.

"What is this? You show me yours and I'll show you mine? We aren't eight."

Her laughter warmed him like sunlight on a frost covered field. "True. But I'd like to know why you're so wary because it doesn't jive with you accepting a ride from a stranger."

"Rides from strangers are kind of a rural-thing. We tend to be a bit less tense around strangers. I think maybe it's the distance between ranches. We're friendly, with a sense of caution thrown in."

They remounted after fastening the wires to the temporary post. She'd neatly avoided answering his question, but he let it go. It seemed they both had some trust issues. He concluded that her hurt must have been more mental than physical. If she'd been physically hurt, she'd have been cautious about taking a ride with him.

"Just around that corner," she said with a wave. "Jack'll be there with a quad."

"One quad?"

"Just one. He can hardly bring two by himself. So, you'll have to ride shotgun while I drive."

"I'll drive," he countered, just to be contrary.

"In a pig's eye you will. My land. My quad. I drive. You've got two choices. Take the horse back with Jack, or ride along."

And ride behind her he did. And it was an enormous mistake. He should have taken the horse back, or walked, or crawled over broken glass, because sitting snugly behind her on the tight confines of the quad was heaven and hell. He spent the next hour and a half repeatedly shifting backward to keep himself from inadvertently rubbing against her backside. And how the hell could the smell of her hair as it blew in his face be so erotic? He was in agony by the time they reached the ranch house and riding horses had nothing to do with his discomfort.

CHAPTER ELEVEN

"Go inside, take a bath," April advised Wade. "A long hot bath. I'll see to the horses. We'll have something to eat and finalize our agreement after that."

"There's no need to rush to a deal," he suggested, slow-stepping his way out of the barn.

He groaned lowly and April resisted the urge to laugh at him. She'd been on the wrong side of an overly enthusiastic ride more than once. Guilt over the torture she'd put him through nagged at her.

"Sorry you're so stiff," she apologized obliquely. "I shouldn't have let you ride like that. I suspected you were somewhat of a greenhorn."

"It's okay. I deserved it. That'll teach me to tell a mistruth."

"A mistruth? Mr. that was an out-and-out lie." She laughed at the color staining his cheeks and gestured toward the house. "Go, soak your tired parts and put some of this on your backside. It'll help." She tossed him a jar of horse liniment; it would sooth his sore muscles, and her conscience.

He glanced at it and stared at her. "This is for animals!"

"It has virtually the same formula as the human one and it's about a tenth of the price. It probably works twice as well. Suck it up and use it. It'll help. And if you can't reach, call Jack. He'll help out."

Half a dozen expressions, including horror, passed over his face before it settled at disappointment. "I'll mange," he mumbled, hobbling away.

Guilt stabbed her again as she noticed the exaggerated care in his motions. She should have left him behind. Taking him on such a long ride was unconscionable, even if she was afraid to go alone. She shouldn't be afraid on her family's land. She should feel free to go wherever she wanted. And without fretting about the possibility of having to use a gun on two-legged varmints.

This wasn't what she'd signed up for when she'd run home with her tail between her legs. She was more than happy to have a place to go to when the shit hit the fan at work. But she needed a sanctuary, not more trouble. Losing her job, her reputation and her fiancé was bad enough, but now she was afraid to be alone on the land she loved. Life sucked some days.

Slowly, deliberately, she brushed down the horses, taking the time to enjoy their company and reward them for the morning's work. She brushed all the occupants of the stable, including the dogs, listening to the comforting sound of Jack hammering away on the roof. Eventually, the pounding stopped. Twenty minutes later, with no distractions remaining, she accepted the inevitable and went inside to prepare lunch. Lord, she missed the days when the ranch had a cook. To her surprise, Jack had lunch ready when she finished washing up.

"Jack, you didn't have to do this," she praised, sliding into a chair at the table.

"It ain't nothin. I was hungry. You were busy," he winked at her, showing that he was aware of her procrastination. "And that greenhorn sure wasn't going to cook. Not in the shape he's in." His voice was laden with censure, ramping up her guilt.

Wade hobbled into the room. "Holy crap. I hurt like hell. I feel like I was run over by a stampede of buffalo."

"Wait 'til tomorrow," Jack laughed. "You won't hardly be able to get outta bed."

Wade groaned.

"Have another bath later, and do some stretches. Five or six batches of them. It'll help. Come, sit," April patted the chair beside her. "Jack's made us lunch."

"I appreciate it. I forgot how hungry riding makes you."

"Well, eat hardy. We've some heavy negotiating to do later."

"WHAT DO YOUR GUESTS PAY? I know you've just arrived and things are in upheaval. But, do you have any idea?" Wade asked.

"Jack told me it varies. And judging by what I saw in the books yesterday, lord, was it only yesterday? Anyway, the longer you stay, the better the deal. We've had people for one night, bed and breakfast style, and apparently for as long as four months. Bale guest are somewhat different."

"Bale?" The term was unfamiliar to Wade.

"Bale. People come for a variety of reasons. Bed and Breakfast people just want a place to stay. Some people want to ride as well, like a dude ranch. Play with the horses and dogs, but refrain from work. Bale guests want the full ranch experience, all the work, chores and tasks, right down to cooking, cleaning and shoveling manure. They want everything. That would be what you want, I think. That rate runs a bit lower than a week as a riding only guest because bale guests work for their keep."

"Okay then, bale rates for a two week stay to start. I want the full cowboy-rancher experience. What's that going to cost me?" It didn't really matter, he had more than enough money to pay whatever she asked; but he was no fool and wouldn't let her overcharge him either.

April named a reasonable sum. Not what she'd charge if the ranch was up to snuff, but reasonable since she'd be putting him to work on rebuilding the place.

"That seems low," he suggested. "I did some research last night on the Internet. You could—no, should, be charging about thirty percent more than that." He wondered why she was undercutting herself; she should ask for more.

"Perhaps, but the Lazy-W isn't exactly a prime vacation spot."

"Valid point." She'd obviously put some thought into the rate. He was impressed. She was already learning from his advice.

"And, if you choose to stay, you'll be working harder than you have ever worked before. Certainly harder than your office job. So, my rate stands. Take it or leave it." Part of her hoped he'd stay, but she also wanted him to leave. He made her uncomfortable. Not in a bad way, but in an oh-my-god-I-want-to-kiss-him way. She could barely sit still waiting for his decision. She made notations on her to-do list. It was a diversion tactic. She already had more chores than she could deal with. But if he stayed…

"I think that price is too low. Let's not cut off your nose to spite your face."

"Take it or leave it," she repeated firmly, thankful her voice didn't betray how much she wanted him to accept.

He stuck out his hand. "Deal. I'll stay two weeks, starting today. And I owe you for yesterday."

"Cheater."

"Take it or leave it," he mocked her before they shook on it. His hand was warm and surprisingly calloused in hers. It felt good. Too good. She like the way her shoulders felt lighter, as if having him there was unburdening her.

"How do you want to be paid? And, I'll need a receipt."

"Cash?" She asked with a wince. "I don't have access to the bank accounts and would prefer not to open another one until I have steady income. Fees…"

"Cash it is. I'll have to go to the bank first."

"We can hit the bank when we go to town, after you check out the truck. I'm sure we'll need parts. Eventually I'll need the money for groceries." She sighed heavily at the admission. Her hands balled into fists on the table. They had some groceries, the ones she'd picked up in town yesterday before her truck broke down. Thankfully the cooler she'd packed the perishables in had kept them fresh until Riley brought the truck home. There were a few vegetables ready for picking in the garden as well. Meat, particularly beef, was never an issue.

"Don't sweat it. Everyone has a tough go at some point. You need to believe you can make this work. There's no shame in being down on your luck. We can get a lot done in a week." He patted her clenched fist.

"Okay," she sighed again. "I'll start a list and prioritize tasks based on urgency and repair cost." She glanced at her watch. "I don't think we'll make the bank today."

He returned to the kitchen an hour later with a list in hand.

"Let's go get these truck parts. We can deduct it from my bill and I'll be able to get that old beast up and running tonight. Unless you had alternate plans for me?"

CHAPTER TWELVE

They returned from town to find eight, twenty-something hipster-looking kids on the porch, arguing with Jack. Jack calmly stood his ground but the youngsters were agitated.

"What seems to be the trouble here?" April strode up to them, struggling to look and feel authoritative. She could smell a crisis brewing; the acid in her stomach starting boiling.

"These folks," Jack sneered at the youngsters, "claim they have a reservation and paid in advance for a seven-day ranch stay."

"We have the paper right here," a girl, who appeared to be their leader, thrust a paper at April.

Wade took the computer printout from her. "Let me have a look at that." He studied it, frowned, and handed it over to April.

"I don't see how this happened," she stalled after perusing what appeared to be a receipt for a fully paid stay. "We don't have an on-line booking system. You'll have to go. We aren't ready for guests."

"And our money? We paid a small fortune to spend seven days here," the spokeswoman declared. "You can't force us to leave." She crossed her arms over her chest, planting her feet like a tree setting down roots.

"Well," Wade drawled, "technically, this is private property and since you are here, uninvited, we can ask you to leave. However," he held up a hand to stall their protests, "give me a moment with my business partner and we'll see what we can do."

April gaped at him but obediently followed him inside. The man had an annoyingly pleasant way of lumping them together as a couple.

"What the heck are you doing?" she blurted out once the door closed. He had no right to take over, even if he had suggested they were equal partners in this venture.

"Be reasonable. These kids paid a lot of money to be here. We can take advantage of that. Feed them and work them. With what I'm paying you, we can afford the food."

"The guest cabins aren't even ready yet. They haven't been used in ages."

"Do they work? Any leaks or issues?"

"No, just dust and dirt. I'd need to freshen the linens, clean the cabins and," she paused mid-sentence. "Maybe this could work. What if we get them to prep the cabins and do other ranch chores?" The idea was feasible, but her guilt gene screamed it was wrong to take advantage of them even though she couldn't afford to refund them money she'd never received.

"Exactly what I was thinking. Free labor."

"It doesn't feel right, using them like that." And it didn't. Guilt plagued her. She was already letting Wade stay under semi-false pretenses. *Can I let these kids stay too? It is dangerous here right now. Red was shot, vehicles have been vandalized. What if I told them the truth? Would they agree to stay? Would they bolt and sue me? I sure as heck couldn't afford to refund the thousands of dollars they paid; especially since I didn't receive it.*

"So, tell them the truth," Wade advised, almost echoing her thoughts. "Give them the choice."

She closed her eyes and struggled for calm. She was wired up, too tense and discomfited to make a rational decision. Pacing back and forth, she considered her options. "We could send them to the RCMP. Have them file a complaint against the website. Because I sure didn't set it up or receive the money."

"Why not both? Let them stay. Let them work, teach them a thing or two about real life and have them file that complaint? Win-win. And I won't mention, until later, that based on what they're paying, I'm going to owe you more money."

"Don't," she warned him. "Don't make this worse. We'll deal with your fees later. But let's do this. Tell them what's up and see what they think?" She meant it to be a statement, but it came out as a question. She was relying on his opinion too much; she'd only just met him. That didn't bode well for the future, or her independence.

"Here's the deal," she said as they returned to the porch. "You've been swindled. I've been swindled."

The group started complaining immediately, everyone talking at once and gesturing wildly.

Wade put his fingers to his lips and whistled shrilly. "Give the woman three minutes to explain before you get upset."

They quieted immediately and let April explain.

"So, you're saying someone set up a bogus website and you can't take us?" the leader asked.

"No, I'm saying that if you want to stay and help pitch in and rebuild the ranch, you are welcome to stay. It'll probably be more work and not the type of work you expected, but we'd love to have you. There'll be good food, plenty of chores, horse riding and a hundred other parts of ranch life to experience. But you also need to know someone shot a bull yesterday. We don't know who or why."

"Can we have some time to think about it?" A short brunette girl stepped forward, taking control from the leader.

"Absolutely. Take all the time you need," April agreed.

The group walked back to their vehicles and stood talking.

"Good lord," April said quietly. "What have I gotten myself into?" She might just have bitten off more than she could chew. Time would tell, she was going to do her best to be optimistic.

"This could be a blessing in disguise. Free labor. And if we make it fun for them, it might lead to more business. Step one in rebuilding the Lazy-W will be underway."

The man was distressingly logical. Why hadn't she seen this? Why hadn't it been her idea? Business was just so far outside her range of experience that it didn't even occur to her. Thank heaven he'd come up with the idea. And if they went to the police, it might convince Miller of the reality of the crap going on here. Who knows, maybe the website would lead to the culprits plaguing her new life.

"We need a plan on where to start," Wade whispered low, his breath tickling her ear.

"What?" She blurted the word loudly. When had he stepped so close?

"If they stay, we need a plan. Where do we start?" He repeated himself.

"Cleaning the cabins and running the stored bedding through the dryer so they'll have a decent place to sleep would be a start. And more groceries."

"So, we split them up. Some of them on housework, and some of them on ranch work. You and Jack can teach them about caring for horses. Tomorrow, if they stay, we'll get them to switch roles. I'm a whiz in the kitchen, so I can run the food."

"We've decided to stay," the brunette proclaimed with a grin. "It's not what we expected, but it'll be an experience. I'm Courtney. Where do we start?"

"I'm April, this is Wade and the cowboy you met earlier is Jack. He's off checking the pregnant cows."

"Oh, I want to help with that," a blond male suggested. "I'm Tommy. Nice to meet you."

They quickly divided the group into two teams and assigned chores.

"Cabins?" Courtney asked when April pointed them in the direction of their new accommodations. "Don't you have a bunkhouse? The website said bunkhouse. That'd be a riot."

"We can do that," April agreed. "But cleaning one cabin, for Jack, is still on the agenda. We'll need to move Jack out of the bunkhouse and into a cabin. I expect he'll want some privacy." Once he was relocated, they'd clean the bunkhouse.

Directions given, April informed Jack of the deal and set

him to work teaching four of them horsemanship. She sent Wade to town with a grocery list, since he had the money he'd pay and they'd deduct if from his bill. She corralled the remaining four and they got started on cleaning.

To April's surprise, the rest of the day went off without a hitch. The kids and April filed a joint complaint with the RCMP about the bogus website. They would issue an order to cease business until they fully investigated the claims of fraud. That done, the kids worked hard and were pleased with the supper they helped make after their chores were done. They loved sitting around the fire listening to Jack tell tall-tales about living on a ranch. The kids had asked permission before bringing out some beer, and willingly forked over IDs. None of them consumed to excess.

Sitting around the kitchen table later, Jack groused a bit about being ousted from the bunkhouse.

"Come on, Jack. You're in a cabin. It's nicer than the bunkhouse by a mile. And you probably don't want to be sharing that big space with a bunch of kids anyway."

"Truer words were never spoken!" he agreed heartily. "But, I'm gonna turn in now. And you," he shook his finger at Wade. "You mind your manners with missy, here." He stuck out his hand abruptly. "Thank you, Wade. Thanks for helping us through this pain-in-the-arse day." They shook hands and he left the room before Wade, or April, could respond.

"Wow. I think Jack likes you." April laughed.

"I never thought I'd see the day," Wade confessed.

"This calls for a celebration. I'll make some tea."

"How about a glass of wine instead?"

"Sadly, there isn't a drop of alcohol in the place. Even Grampa Morgan's secret Scotch stash is gone."

"Hold tight. I have a bottle in my truck."

"You brought wine?" Her words landed on his retreating back.

He returned with two bottles, one white, one red, before she had the dust rinsed off the glasses. They opened the white, a Pinot Gris from a British Columbia vineyard.

"A toast to turning a sow's ear into a silk purse," she proposed raising her glass and laughing at the startled expression on his face.

"To a job well done and a disaster averted," he amended.

They touched glasses and sipped.

"We make a good team, you and I."

She studied him for a moment, sipping slowly to allow time to think. The wine was smooth and tart on her tongue. Tasty. They did make a good team. Too bad his presence here was only temporary. She could use a partner to help get things done. Too bad their life paths were so different. He appeared to be a high-profile businessman. She was a poverty-stricken woman with temporary hold on a dilapidated ranch. He was city; she was country. And she didn't even want to think about being wrongfully fired from her last job, thanks to her jackass ex. Nope, friendship was all they'd ever have. The man would cut and run the minute he realized she was carrying another man's baby.

"That was a big sigh," he said quietly. "You drifted away for a minute there."

"Yeah," she puffed out a disgruntled breath and set the wine down. "Suddenly it just seems like too much."

"Have a drink. Relax. We had a fabulous day."

"I can't." She pushed the wine away and went to the sink.

Drawing a large glass of water, she took several sips, standing with her back to him.

"Sorry you opened the wine for nothing." *Please, please, please, don't let him ask questions. Fat chance! He isn't the type to let questions go unanswered.*

"Well, I intend to enjoy mine, even if you don't drink yours." He paused. "Care to tell me why you had such a sudden change of heart."

"I'd prefer not to, thanks."

His chair shifted and she heard him move closer. His hands, warm and gentle came to rest on her shoulders.

"What is it?" he asked, turning her around to face him. His finger brushed across her cheek. "You're crying?"

"Sorry," she sniffed and tried to push out of reach. "I'll be fine, I'm just a bit emotional. Today's been one hell of a ride. I feel like I just went ten rounds on a prize-winning bull."

"Bull is right. Bull shit." His voice was soft and gentle, in contrast to the harsh words.

She didn't look up. She shifted on her feet, trying to find a way to escape him without touching him.

"I know we aren't best friends," he said. "Hell, we hardly know each other. But you can talk to me. What's bothering you? I'm perplexed. You seemed excited about the wine, and suddenly you don't want any. Does someone you know have an alcohol addiction?"

"No. I just..." She looked over his shoulder. There wasn't any sense lying about this. His eyes told her he'd just keep pressing the issue until she told him. "Dang. I'm pregnant. My ex-husband was a lying, cheating, no good bastard. He doesn't know I'm pregnant and he never will. Okay? I'm a single woman carrying a baby and I shouldn't be drinking."

She moved away, waiting for the recriminations, for the fallout of her announcement. If he wasn't leery about being around the ranch before, this would tip him over the edge.

"You're trying to run this place alone? And you're pregnant? Are you insane? A woman alone can't run a ranch this size. It's more work than two people can handle, let alone when one is carrying a child. Kudos to you for trying. Care to tell me how you got in this position?"

Strangely accusatory and compassionate at the same time, his response cut into her. Self-recrimination washed over her. Why had she let herself get pregnant? No, the real question was why had she married such a jackass? Eventually she responded. "I got pregnant the usual way," she said wryly.

He chuckled. "I gathered that. But I was more curious about your story with your ex."

"We met, fell in love, got married. He turned out to be a jerk. I divorced his cheating ass." She was not getting into the fact that she'd had a few drinks and slept with her ex in a moment of weakness.

"And that's how you ended up on the Lazy-W? Homeless and jobless, I think you said. Was he involved in your career change?"

"Wow, you cut to the chase, don't you? I really prefer not to talk about it. I hadn't even intended to tell you. I was going to keep my mouth shut. Before long, you'd be gone and none the wiser. So, we'll just let it go and pretend we never had this conversation." *Yeah, fat chance that he'll agree to that.*

"Okay. I'll give you your privacy. It is none of my business. I'm not saying I'm disinterested, I'm curious as hell. But, because you asked me to let it drop, I will. Do note, however, I'm dropping it under protest. If you ever want to talk about it, to work things out in your mind, let me know. I've been told I'm a good listener. I applaud your decision to avoid alcohol and I'm not in the least offended that you choose not to drink it. I'll drink it on your behalf." He chuckled. "I'll call it a personal sacrifice—for me." He smiled broadly and laughed again.

"Big of you." She laughed with him; his smile was contagious. "Thanks for understanding."

CHAPTER THIRTEEN

The persistent dinging of her cell phone alerted April that it was morning. The phone was her last luxury and if she wasn't locked into a contract, it would be long gone. As it was, she'd reduced service to almost nothing.

"Good gravy," she groaned, rolling over to silence the alarm. "It's way too early to get up." She tossed back the covers and swung her feet over the bed in one smooth motion. Her stomach lurched alarmingly. Snatching her robe off the hook on the back of the door, she bolted downstairs to the bathroom and heaved into the toilet.

"What the hell?" she muttered, cleaning herself up and rinsing her mouth with mouthwash. She'd gone three months without a single bout of morning sickness. Why now?

A soft knock sounded on the door. "April? Are you okay? Is it just morning sickness? Or is it more serious? Is there anything I can do?" Wade asked through the door.

"Go away," she groaned. Her stomach heaved again, she slipped into the robe she'd dropped on the floor before she got sick.

"Small sips of water, and try nibbling soda crackers before you get out of bed. Sometimes sips of flat ginger ale help too," he advised, seeming to ignore her surly mood. "Do you have ginger ale? Should I go to town and get some?"

She jerked the door open to glare at him. "What made you such an expert on pregnancy? Got a wife I don't know about?" *Oh crap, why'd I go and ask that? Blame it on my upset stomach and the ungodly early hour.*

Wade let loose a full belly-laugh. Eventually, her glare silenced him. "No wife, but I do find it curious that you want to know. Where was that question when I first showed up?"

"I don't care what your marital status is. You are a guest here, nothing more, nothing less." She squeezed past him and headed for the stairs. "I'll be back to cook, after I get dressed."

Changing clothes took longer than she had anticipated. Visions of Wade standing in her bathroom doorway, loose pajama bottoms slung low on his hips, his chest and feet bare, were creating shock waves of hormones and wreaking havoc with her equilibrium. It had taken every ounce of her reserve to keep her hands to herself. It must be the pregnancy hormones making her susceptible to his manly charms. Yeah. That was it!

The heavenly aroma of coffee hit her smack dab in the gag reflex as she descended the stairs. She could do this; she could get beyond this urge to puke. She had to. She had a bunkhouse full of guests to feed.

Wade and the two guests assigned to breakfast duty had things well under control. April set the table and assisted where she could. Slowly, the remaining guests trickled in. The room bubbled with pleasant conversation and talk of the day's plans. It reminded her of a morning break back at the hospital. Everyone chatting and enjoying themselves. But that was her old life; before she was framed for drug thefts and subsequently fired.

With one group dispatched to look after cattle with Jack, the remaining guests joined Wade and April on a visual survey of the buildings and boardwalks to determine which needed repairs, what they had the materials to repair, and which were the most crucial.

They walked through the yard, and April stopped to pick a dandelion in full seed. Closing her eyes, she made a wish and blew the seeds away.

"Don't ranchers hate dandelions?" Wade asked. "Aren't they a weed?"

"They're a weed, and some call them a pain in the butt. However, I love them. So pretty when they're in bloom, like drops of sunshine in the grass. And when they go to seed, they're blow-flowers. You make a wish and blow the seeds away and they carry your wishes with them." She laughed. The idea was silly, but she'd believed it since her grandmother had told her about it when April was a small child. She wasn't about to stop believing now, when she needed good luck more than at any other time in her life.

"That explains the pot of dandelions in the kitchen window." He grinned. "I've been wondering about them."

Two hundred yards from the house, just outside the main yard, was a rundown guest cabin. It was unsuitable for renting out, and one side of the roof was falling in. The walls and beams were barely sound enough to hold up what was left. For now. The windows and doors were gone, but there was plenty of good wood for repairing the walkways and the remains of the tin roof could be salvaged for repairs on other buildings when the need arose. Loaded up with tools, and rope lines that enabled them to work safely, the small group adopted a divide and conquer mentality and began cautious demolition.

"April, where would I find an old bucket? Maybe a five-gallon pail. If we had a bin of some sort for the used nails, it would save on cleanup later," one of the guests asked.

April paused, halfway up the ladder to the roof. "In the shop, there must be a bunch of empties. Grampa Morgan never threw away anything that might come in handy."

Wade rounded the corner. "Get off that ladder, this instant."

"I beg your pardon?" She stared down at him with one raised eyebrow.

"Get. Off. That. Ladder. Now."

Four pairs of interested eyes turned toward them and all work stopped.

"I will not. I have a building to tear down."

"Yes, *we* do," he emphasized the pronoun. "You can work at ground level. Pregnant women have no place scaling ladders. It isn't safe."

She slid down the ladder and whirled on him. "First, this is my place. You can't tell me what to do. Second, I'm not going to fall off the roof. I'll tie myself down. Third, pregnant women can do anything men can do. Fourth, I'm not a moron. Mind your own damned business." She expected a response. When none was forthcoming, she returned to the ladder.

"I apologize," he said quietly. "Technically, you're right. This isn't any of my business. But I would hate to see something happen to you or your baby. Please let someone else do the ladder work."

Her face must have been red. The male guests sucked in their breaths as if expecting an explosion. The girls sighed blissfully. April glared at all of them before looking at Wade.

"You're right," she sighed. "For a moment, I'd actually forgotten I'm pregnant. I'll stay off the ladder. But, in the future, I'll thank you to avoid taking me to task in front of other people."

"Again, I apologize. My foster-sister Micah calls me a Neanderthal. I can't help myself. I'm genetically programmed to take care of women."

"Dude," Jeff, one of the guests, said with a groan.

"It's not like that," Wade backpedaled. "It isn't chauvinistic. Well, mostly not. I think everyone deserves the right to try and do whatever they want to. I made my business a success when a lot of people didn't think I'd make it. It worked because I tried and overcame the odds. My sister did too. Everyone has that opportunity, but men and women are not equal." He held up his hand in a stop motion. "I run a business. I hire based on qualifications and nothing else. Three out of five of my top executives are women. They're the best at what they do."

He paused. "But, overall, I believe men and women have different skills, different abilities. There are exceptions, but I think the male brain and the female brain differ. It's what makes the species work. Different, but equal and complimentary. Does that make any sense at all? I'm not explaining it well."

"I never thought of it like that," April murmured. "It makes sense. Men and women do seem to think differently.

And certainly, as a rule, men are physically stronger. Equal but different…I like it."

"Thank goodness, I was expecting an argument." He chuckled. "It's not chauvinist, it's not feminist. I think of it as…humanist. As for helping women, that's part and parcel of standing up for anyone who is weaker than yourself or who might need a helping hand. But babies? Babies are precious cargo. Small, fragile, they need the best care they can get. And I'm sticking up for the gift you carry."

"Thank you," April said softly and smiled at him. Good gravy, he was melting her heart. She should be angry at him for sticking his nose in her business, but she wasn't. That was weird, because if her ex had tried to order her around, she'd have told him off and done what she wanted anyway. Perhaps that was because her ex, Stan, never explained what went on in his head. He just handed out orders. But Wade, oh good lord, Wade was kind and helpful. He acted like he was Prince Charming and she was the fairy tale princess. He had, she admitted, a cowboy kind of charm. Not too shabby for a city slicker.

He'd rushed to her rescue so many times already and she'd only known him for days. A girl could get used to being treated like she was important. But to have him stand up for another man's baby? She almost fanned herself and swooned. So hot, so sexy. And so not what she needed right now.

"Hello?" A male voice carried down the path from the main yard. "Hello? I'm looking for April Cooper."

She turned toward the man standing at the edge of the grass. A suit and tie? A briefcase? *And was that a vest? Good gravy.* Now what? Just when things were starting to look up, fresh trouble came calling. She was getting mighty sick of it.

"That's me." She waved and started toward him. She glanced at the guests. "You guys get started. Hopefully, this won't take long."

"I'm with you," Wade interjected, stepping up to walk beside her.

"I'm April. What can I do for you?" She stopped several strides away from the stranger.

"I'm Kurt Werner." He offered his hand. "I'd like to talk to you. Alone." He gave Wade a significant look.

"And what is it that you need to talk about?" she asked, ignoring his rudeness and his outstretched hand. Something about him rubbed her the wrong way.

"It's a private matter." He sniffed and tilted his chin up, dropping the hand she'd refused to shake.

WADE STARED AT KURT. He knew the name Kurt Werner but couldn't recall where he'd heard it. The guy had the look of an ambulance chaser. Cheaply made three-piece suit. Stained tie, battered briefcase, scuffed shoes. If he was trying to make a good impression, he was failing.

"Would you like me to leave?" Wade asked April, resting one hand on her shoulder. It tensed under his touch. Something was up here. She was so nervous she was almost trembling.

"No. Anything Mr. Werner wishes to discuss can be said with you here." Her left hand came up to cover his where it rested on her right shoulder. Her fingers were trembling.

Wade doubted Werner would notice, but she gripped Wade's hand tightly.

"Can we go inside at least?" Werner requested. His shoulders rose and he shifted from foot to foot. His gaze darted everywhere, except to April.

Nervous, is he? Interesting. Why should he be nervous?

"Certainly," April agreed. "Let's go to the house. We can talk there." She grabbed Wade's hand and they stepped past Werner, leaving him trailing behind them, hurrying to catch up.

"So," Wade asked once they were settled at the kitchen table. "What can we do for you?"

"And you are?" Werner growled dismissively. "You look familiar. Do I know you?"

"I don't think I know you," Wade hedged. "I'm April's advisor," he offered in his best Lord-of-the-Manor voice. He wasn't about to let this man push April around.

"Is that true?" Werner's gaze flashed between April and Wade. "I wasn't informed you had an advisor." He clamped his mouth shut as if he hadn't meant to divulge that.

"As it happens, he is my advisor." She flicked her fingers dismissively. "Go on. What is it you needed to see me about?"

Wade almost laughed at her attitude. She was tough, putting on a show, hiding her trepidation.

Werner straightened his shoulders and puffed out his chest. "I represent a party who's interested in purchasing the Lazy-W. They wish to offer you a substantial amount of money." Setting his briefcase on the table, he flipped it open.

"Indeed." Wade smirked and raised one eyebrow. "And how much might that be?"

"Ms. Cooper, are you sure you want him here?" Werner flipped nervously through the papers in his briefcase.

"Mr. Werner, finish this up." She gestured for him to hurry it along, and he named a substantial sum of money.

"You expect me to sell the Lazy-W?"

"As I said, this is a very generous offer," he repeated the purchase offer.

"I'm not good with math," Wade lied. "How much is that per acre?"

"Well, there are two full sections of land, plus the outbuildings and fences and twenty leased quarters, for a total of four thousand four hundred eighty acres. Understand that leased quarters aren't as valuable as owned quarters. My client has no interest in raising cattle. The leased quarters will be disposed of."

"What I understand is you're offering far under market value for the ranch," Wade interrupted.

"I'd like to see the offer," April suggested.

"Unfortunately, I'm unable to show it to you unless you agree to sign it first."

"That's ridiculous and probably illegal." April frowned. "Let me see it and I'll consider the offer." She waggled her fingers, encouraging Werner to pass the paperwork over.

"Acceptance first, then you can see it." Werner crossed his arms over his chest.

"Not happening. I have no interest in selling the ranch. Thank you."

Werner looked pleadingly at April. "Ms. Cooper, you should reconsider."

"No, thank you. I won't deal with secretive buyers. You can tell your investors the Lazy-W is not for sale." She stood, pushing her chair back.

Wade followed suit. "Let me walk you to the door."

Werner placed a business card on the table. "Call me if you change your mind. We understand you are in financial difficulty. We were just trying to help out."

He returned to the kitchen to find April laughing hysterically. "Oh, my God, I had no idea this place was worth that much money. Not that I would sell it, or that I could sell it."

"Actually, it's worth at least double what he offered, based on today's market," Wade corrected. "I own some land, not productive land like this place, but it does give me the value for this area and he is low-balling you, big-time. Either he thinks you are stupid, or he's up to something. Either way, he'd trying to take advantage of you."

"I couldn't sell it, not that I want to. I don't own it. Right now, nobody does. There's a mortgage on it that's in arrears, but my uncle is missing. So is my grandfather's will. Nobody knows what's going on and I can't afford a lawyer to sort things out." She sighed.

"So, your uncle's been gone how long?"

"About a year. He was running the ranch, sort of, for close to six years. Or rather five. Grampa Morgan's been gone six, and Uncle John disappeared about a year ago. Dad died shortly after Grampa and, with the will missing…" she trailed off.

"Everything's in limbo. You're right, you couldn't sell it even if you wanted to. What's the bank's take on all of this? I'm sure they've been after you for outstanding payments."

"There wasn't anything due until Uncle John took over. Now we owe about two hundred thousand dollars. They gave me six months to start making payments, but the interest accrues as we speak. I'm already two months into that, so four months left."

"Four months is good and bad. That's a long time to accrue interest, but lots of time to get the ranch up and running and the land alone is worth a lot more than that."

"I'd like to know who told him I needed money. That doesn't make sense. It isn't as if he can just look me up on the Internet and find out my financial status. Can he?" Doubt filled her voice.

"He can't. Financial institutions can delve into your business under certain circumstances, but it's more likely someone is after the ranch for reasons of their own and did some background checking. A lot can be inferred from random tidbits of information. It might just be an educated guess. In truth, if you have the right investigator, discovering a person's secrets isn't difficult. Or so I hear."

"Well, he's not getting the ranch from me, not if I can help it. I just have to get things up and running again. So, back to work for me." She smiled and stood. "Thanks for helping with that."

"I have a friend, he's a lawyer. I could ask him to consider this for you and see what options are open. He does some pro-bono work, so there wouldn't be much of a fee."

"How much is not much?"

"If it's okay with you, I'll have him come out and talk to you and discuss options. And fees." *And Wade would invite him, right after he told his top corporate and personal lawyer he was now doing pro-bono work. Or rather pretending to do pro-bono work and billing it to Wade.*

"I guess that would be okay. But can you make sure there isn't a fee for him to come out? Please."

Wade agreed readily, hating the shame and dismay in her voice. Why did he keep stepping in? The strength of his attraction to April was bewildering. She was strong and fragile. Independent and capable, yet needy. No, not needy. In need and struggling to cope. Was her magnetism because she resisted the urge to depend on others, instead seeming to prefer standing on her own two feet? She'd cried a few times over the loss of loved ones but kept strong and stoic over the other issues she'd encountered since he arrived. Strong and soft was a deadly combination.

She was different from most of the socialite women he knew. Her independence was refreshing. Add that to her obvious and oft repeated reluctance to accept his money and she stood miles apart from the usual society gold-digger. None of his close friends, male or female, fit the rich, greedy and needy mold; but he knew enough people like that to realize the stereotype existed for a reason. Sadly, the woman he'd once planned to marry fit firmly into the gold-digger category. He was lucky to have discovered her dark side before the wedding.

"Why does a developer want a chunk of land in the middle of nowhere?" Wade blurted, hiding his own desire to purchase a ranch for his corporate retreat. "Is there anything special here? Minerals? Hot springs? Old growth forest for timber? Anything? You don't have a secret plutonium mine, do you?"

"There's only a bit of big timber. Most was logged years ago. No minerals. Well, there are a couple oil wells and a tiny mineral spring that's more like a warm-ish spring that pours into a rock-lined pool created by one of my ancestors. But it's hardly bigger than a hot tub. There isn't anything of value here, except the cattle and the land itself. Even the buildings have seen better days, in case you hadn't noticed."

"That makes this doubly odd." From a business perspective, Werner's offer was ridiculous and suspicious. It made Wade wonder if the anonymous purchaser had a hidden agenda.

"Especially when you add in the damage to my truck, the tractor and someone shooting Red. Something's going on here and I sure wish I knew what it was." She scrubbed her face with her palms.

"Geological surveys might help identify something. We can do a basic lookup on the Internet and if we think it's necessary, have a comprehensive one paid for, though almost everything is available on the government's public site."

CHAPTER FOURTEEN

"April? Jack says he needs you down at the horse paddock." Betsy, one of the guests, informed April later that afternoon.

April slid her hammer into the loop on her tool belt and stuck her head out the cabin door. "What's up?"

"Two of the horses are acting sick. He says they've got colic. Isn't colic a baby thing. My nephew has colic. I didn't know horses could get it." She sounded bewildered.

"It's a baby thing." April laughed. "Technically, colic means upset stomach or stomach pain." She frowned. "But in a horse, colic can be deadly. It's usually the sign of something else." She turned to address the group working on the cabin. "You guys keep working on the demolition. I have to go see a man about a horse." April slapped a hand over her mouth, realizing the double meaning of her words. It had been years since she heard a ranch hand use that expression.

"Indeed?" Wade quipped. "Isn't that what you were doing when I met you?"

Betsy's gaze flew back and forth between them. "What are you talking about?" Betsy asked.

"Nothing." Heat rose in April's face.

"It's an old expression for peeing outside, or leaving the room to use the washroom. But I think, in this case, she actually meant it literally." Wade chuckled. "Come on. Let's go talk to Jack." He waved April forward.

"Pretty sure I can handle this on my own. And, I'm certain you don't know a danged thing about colic. You barely know anything about horses. Why don't you stay and supervise?"

"Can we come?" Courtney, the leader of the guests, asked. "We are here to learn about ranching, and Tommy's fascinated by the horses."

April winced and suppressed a sigh. It was easy to see that balancing guests and ranch disasters was going to be an epic juggling act. In for a penny, in for a pound. Or misery loved company. "Come on then, let's go see what we can do. Follow me, but you'll have to stay back and keep quiet. A colicky horse is in agony and they're nervous and flighty and likely to kick or bite."

Mustard and Salty Dog showed all the symptoms of colic, which didn't make any sense. Colic typically came from bad feed and Jack was scrupulously careful about what the horses were fed. There was no option but to call in the vet. Aki arrived in short order.

She listened to their stomachs, checked their vital signs and did a rectal exam. The diagnosis was clear. Colic. It had come on quickly enough that it couldn't be an accident. It had to be deliberate. Two of April's horses had been poisoned.

Using a nasogastric-stomach tube, she administered

medication to alleviate the gas and bloating before calling the RCMP to inform them the horses had been poisoned. She had finished caring for the horses, leaving April and Jack to walk the pair, preventing them from lying down and exacerbating their agony. She said her good-byes and walked back to her truck.

"HI, WADE," Aki said with a broad welcoming smile.

"Hi. What do we need to do to care for them?" He asked, ignoring the vet's flirtatious smile. Admittedly the woman was attractive, but she just didn't move him. Normally, her exotic beauty would be appealing, but today, all he could think about was April's golden hair and lightly tanned skin.

"Want to get a beer sometime?" Aki asked after giving Wade instructions on dealing with colic.

"Thanks, but no."

"You and April a thing?" she queried.

"No. Just friends." He wasn't interested in Aki, but didn't want to be rude.

Aki laughed at that. "Go ahead, tell yourself that. But you can't keep your eyes off her and you're never more than three feet from her side. You, Wade Kelly Borne, are smitten."

His eyes bulged at the disclosure of his full name. "How did you know?" He'd been hoping to keep his identity hidden for longer than this, but apparently that plan had failed. "I don't suppose you'll keep this to yourself?"

"You seemed familiar to me when I was out here after the death of the bull," the vet said meaningfully, "and then this morning your face made the news. An article in the paper about your company and a Christmas party you put on every year for sick kids." She smiled at him. "I don't know why you're keeping your identity a secret, but your secret's safe with me for now. But, if you hurt my friend…" she grinned evilly and shrugged, punching him in the chest. "Suffice it to say, I have a medical background and can make it look like an accident." She laughed.

Wade blinked in surprise. "Are you threatening me?"

"Not at all," she smiled, licking her lips. "You must have misunderstood. Look, Wade, I don't know what's up, but I'll give you the benefit of the doubt. For now." She packed up her gear and climbed into her truck. "Tell April I'll send a bill. And if you change your mind about that beer…" she winked, then left the words dangling and drove away.

It dawned on him that none of the kids had recognized him. They couldn't spend much time watching the news or reading the paper. Oh well, if they did know who he was, they'd have mentioned it by now.

Hours later, Wade watched April pace the kitchen, furious. "I can't believe Miller thinks we'd poison our own horses for the insurance money. He's out of his cotton-picking mind. If we wanted the money, we'd never have called the vet. Not that there is any insurance. Uncle John let that lapse right after he arrived." She sighed. "Grampa had life insurance, enough to bury him, I think. But anything on the land, buildings or cattle is long since cancelled."

"Something's not right with Miller. He's all over the map. Agreeing, disagreeing. He's too quick with accusations. I've been around cops before but, typically, they give a person the benefit of the doubt."

"His son was doing drugs," Jack offered. "Before he went

AWOL from the military. Nobody's seen the boy for months. Maybe that's throwing Miller off and he's too stressed to do his job?"

"Whatever the reason," April said with a sigh, "he's driving me nuts. He's making me crazier than a coyote with its tail caught in a trap."

CHAPTER FIFTEEN

"What's the plan for today, Boss?" Wade asked after the group had finished another delicious breakfast of bacon, scrambled eggs, waffles, toast and fruit salad. The scent of fresh coffee hung in the air like ambrosia.

"Fences. We need to check the entire perimeter. That's eleven miles of slow going on a quad, but it's a nice ride. Grampa Morgan had a rule about keeping a wide clearing around the perimeter fences. Wide enough for a quad at least."

"If it's clear around the perimeter, what happened to the fences we rode the other day on horseback?" Wade asked.

"Those were interior fences. Some of them aren't as accessible. They're important, but not critical. If a cow wanders from one pasture to another, it's not a big deal. But escaping the ranch altogether can be a pain in the hinny. I suppose your butt still hurts?" she teased.

He wiggled his hips and did a couple of squats. "Nope, all good here. I'm ready to ride again. I rode a bit yesterday. That helped loosen me up."

"Good thinking. I should have suggested that." April smiled at him.

Wade Kelly was something else. Cheerful, he didn't complain and was more than willing to pull his weight around the ranch. April had only known him three days and already she felt dependent on him; and that was a feeling she didn't care for. Hopefully, she'd be able to get back on her feet before he disappeared into the rain he'd come from. And hopefully, he'd be gone before she fell for him. Her heart couldn't take the strain of another doomed relationship.

"Okay people," she called out. "Someone will have to ride the fence, plus check and repair any broken posts or lose wires. All the gates need to be closed and latched and we need to check for signs of traffic."

"Traffic?" someone asked.

"There shouldn't be any vehicles on the Lazy-W. So, any tracks, from vehicles or quads, need to be investigated. Someone was close enough to give the horses bad feed. We need to determine how they got in. It's unlikely they came in by the front gate, although they might have walking in during the night."

Running a ranch had never seemed this difficult when she was a kid, not even when she accounted for the fact kids tended to be oblivious to the undercurrents of things happening around them. Additionally, back then, it didn't feel like someone had it in for the ranch. Good gravy, one of the horses might have died if they didn't have guests to share the work. Jack might have just left the horses at pasture that day instead of checking on them. Too many weird things were happening. But at least there hadn't been any more gunfire. Lord love a duck, she just wanted things back to normal.

The crew shifted restlessly, drawing her attention back to them.

"Sorry about that." She grinned. "Lost in thought for a second. Have any of you ever used a chainsaw?" she asked. "You might have to remove fallen trees from the fence lines. Small ones are easily moved, but the big ones are an entirely different issue."

Nobody responded, except to shake their heads negatively.

"Okay then," she replied with a smile. "I guess the chain sawing is up to Jack and me. Make note of anywhere you find a tree on the fence-line and any nearby landmarks. If the fence is completely down, let us know right away, please. We don't want any cows making the great getaway. We'll go back later to repair the ones that aren't an immediate problem. Feel free to call my cell or Wade's if you have any difficulties, but it's a pretty straightforward job."

She answered a few questions and, after providing them with hand-drawn maps, she dispatched four students on two quads with the tools they needed to fix the fences.

"You sure you're doing the right thing?" Jack asked once they were alone in the kitchen. "Them kids are as green as grass. Mark my words, there'll be trouble. They ain't got the skills for this," he grumbled, staring into his coffee.

"That's neither here nor there. They might be city kids, but they're smart enough to recognize a broken fence. They might not get the job done, but they're learning about ranching and that's why they came here. Grampa had Bale guests doing chores like this all the time. Besides, it frees me up to help you check for stray calves."

"I still don't like it, back then, we had plenty of hands to keep 'em in line. We could check them fences while we checked the calves," he muttered.

"Jack, be reasonable," she implored. "We've got seven sections of land. That's twenty-eight quarters. Seven square miles of ground to cover. Two people can't do that alone in a reasonable time frame. If every area was accessible by quad, it would be a different story, but much of the brush is too dense for that and you know it. I won't even mention the rocky areas. Last time I was here, Grampa Morgan had ten hands, including you. Admittedly, we don't have nearly as many cattle, or horses, but we'll accept their help and be glad of it."

"You know, there was a time when I'd have turned you over my knee for backtalk like that," he said fondly. "But you're the boss now and we'll do as you say. It ain't right, though. You being a woman alone and looking after this place."

She leaned in and kissed his whiskered cheek before hugging him. "I'm not alone, Jack. I've got you, and I'd be lost without you. And those kids are lightening the load, too. We're going to make it work. I can feel it in my bones."

"I dang well hope so. We best get ahead enough that we can hire another hand before you set to havin' that baby of yours. Unless Wade intends to hang around," he said.

She almost laughed at the blend of hope and dismay in his voice at the idea of Wade becoming a permanent fixture. She felt precisely the same way, though she'd never admit to falling for Wade, not even to herself; though having him here was a comfort. And a strain.

"I hope we're in better shape before the baby comes. Now, we better get going." She finished the last sip of her coffee and headed for the barn.

A warm pine-scented breeze blew away the clouds, leaving only wisps of white in a perfect blue sky. The sun was up and the day was starting to heat up already. The morning promised to turn into a beautiful day. Charlie Chaplin and Chives were the horses for today's chores. It was two hours of steady riding before they discovered anything amiss.

"Listen," April called out, reigning her horse to a slower trot. "Do you hear that?"

Jack nodded and they followed a calf's bellowing until they located her and her downed mother.

"What the hell?" April blurted out, dismounting quickly, staring at the mangled cow at her feet. The cow lay in a pool of bloody mud at the edge of a thicket of brush. Her bawling calf stood, nearby.

The cow hadn't been injured or attacked by another animal. She'd been slaughtered. Her throat was slit; her intestines spilled from a straight slice across her abdomen, trailing all over the ground. She hadn't been dead long. Scavengers hadn't even started on her corpse, though crows were beginning to circle high overhead.

In the nearby woods, April heard the rustling of something moving stealthily through the bush. A coyote howled and was answered by several high-pitched yips. The sound sent shivers down April's spine. Hungry predators were dangerous. She didn't need this. Not now. She'd been hoping to sell some calves to finance ranch operations. Losing a cow was a financial blow they didn't need. Who would do something like this, and why? She glanced around her, searching the nearby brush and field for two legged predators. Her shoulders tingled and the hair on the back of her neck stood up. She couldn't shake the feeling that someone was watching them.

"Cut off her tag for the records and lasso that calf. We need to take the calf back to the main yard before whatever's in that brush decides to make a meal of one of us. Better that they should eat this cow than that calf. Dammit. I should have brought the rifle."

"That would've been damn stupid. With so many untrained kids running around this place, you could shoot one of them by mistake."

"Unlikely, but I get the point. After today, nobody leaves the yard unarmed. If they aren't familiar with proper gun safety, they'll be unarmed but accompanied by one of us who is. This cow's been murdered. It's a deliberate act of sabotage. Another one." She yanked out her phone and started photographing the scene. "There's barely a boot print around here, although the calf's hoofs would have ground any tracks into oblivion. That's a knife wound, and there aren't any claw or teeth marks I can see. This was done by a rotten, no good, yellow-bellied coward. I can't even call them human. We would never have known she was gone until we took a head count, then we'd chalk her up to scavenger loss. And we could've lost the calf too."

Finished photographing the scene, she slammed the phone into her pocket and jerked it back out when it rang.

"April," she answered briskly. She listened for a moment. "What?" she yelped into the phone. "Where are you? We'll be right there. Hold tight and put pressure on it."

Her heart froze and then stuttered into motion, pounding double-time. Her mouth went dry and she struggled to swallow the lump of panic rising in her throat. She was a nurse, for Pete's sake. She should be able to handle this! God, she'd been so stupid letting those kids stay here, with everything going on. She was to blame for this. How was she ever going to live with herself if Tommy died?

She had medical training! Right. She had to get to him. Immediately! She could mitigate the damages and save him. She bolted to her horse and jumped into the saddle. "Come on, Jack. We've got to go. Tommy's been shot!"

She thundered ahead of him, riding as fast as she dared, opening gates without dismounting and leaving Jack to close them behind her. The ride was short, just under two miles to where Courtney said they were, but time slowed to an eternity and it seemed like she was riding through molasses and would never arrive.

She reigned in Charlie Chaplin and dismounted with an ungraceful stumble. Panting with exhaustion and dripping sweat, the horse gasped for air.

"What happened," she blurted, dropping to her knees beside Tommy, who lay on his back in the grass moaning in pain. The copper scent of fresh blood scraped her nostrils and she bit back a gag.

Courtney kneeled beside Tommy, putting pressure on the front and back of his thigh.

"There was a crack, like gunfire, and he just dropped, clutching his leg. The hole isn't very big. Everyone else freaked out and took off back to the main yard," Courtney blurted. "I wanted to go, but I had to stay for Tommy."

"Good thinking. We want everyone safe. The main yard's the safest place we have. How bad is his leg?" April asked, striving to remain calm. She was on the verge of panic.

Everything she knew as a nurse had vanished when she got the call.

"The bleeding has mostly stopped. Through and through. I think," Courtney said.

"Through and through?" April forced a chuckle to ease the tension of the dire situation. "Watch a lot of police dramas, do you?"

Courtney groaned. "I might never watch another one after this."

"Let me look," April nudged Courtney aside gently, her fingers shaking. "I'm a nurse." The conversation had taken only seconds, but it felt like hours. She was twitchy and overanxious.

Cautiously, she took over applying pressure to Tommy's leg and then slowly peeked under the bandage. He moaned. The bleeding *had* almost completely stopped. He'd need some medical attention and they'd have to notify the RCMP, but it looked like he'd be okay.

"How much blood has he lost?" she asked, seeking confirmation of her diagnosis. There was only a small amount of blood on the ground.

"Not too much, I think." Her voice shook with the aftershock of the incident. "I put pressure on where it went in, and where it came out.

April shifted out of her light coat and covered Tommy with it. "Jack," she addressed the breathless cowboy as he dismounted. "I need a rag or something to put on this." She turned back to Tommy. "How you holding up, kiddo?"

"It hurts like bloody-fucking-hell," he grumbled. "But I'll live." Then he flashed the biggest grin she'd ever seen. "I can't wait to get home and tell my buddies I got shot. This is gonna make an epic story. I'll win the strange-but-true vacation story contest for sure and I'll have the scars to prove it! Fuck, that hurt," he cried out when April threaded her belt under his leg and buckled it around the clean bandana Jack produced from his pocket.

"I'll call Wade and get him to drive his truck out here," April stated. "Hopefully he can make it close enough without getting stuck. We'll take Tommy to the Triangle Grove and meet him there." Once she had him on the phone, April walked Wade through the twisted, convoluted path to get to Triangle Grove, a ranch landmark, without risking damage to his truck. They loaded Tommy on the quad and cautiously drove him to the grove.

A low, stabbing pain slammed into her abdomen and she barely held back a groan.

Dammit. She'd ridden too hard. She should have taken it easy. She had a baby to consider. But how did you choose between your baby and a stranger needing help? It hadn't been a conscious choice; she'd reacted to the emergency as she always would. *Dammit.*

"Jack's got the horses. Can you take the quad back to the main yard, please?" April addressed Courtney after Wade arrived, trying not to alarm anyone about her condition, trying to remain in control of the emergency. "I'll need you to meet us at the hospital in Edson to file a police report."

They loaded Tommy into the truck and headed into town. Sergeant Miller was meeting them at the hospital to take their statements. April swallowed, feeling another stab of pain. Maybe it was time to sell the ranch. She didn't know which was worse, the pain in her belly, or the one in her heart.

CHAPTER SIXTEEN

Another of the continual waves of pain slashed through April as she stood in the waiting room, waiting for word on Tommy. She dropped into a chair, gasping for breath, clutching her belly. *Okay, this is worrisome. I shouldn't still be cramping. If it was just the stress from the fast ride, it should have settled by now.* There were times when having medical training had its disadvantages.

Wade whirled around to look at her. "What's wrong? You're pale," he demanded kindly.

"Nothing. I'm good," she lied and groaned when another debilitating wave hit her. She was not going to admit she might have overdone it. She was a nurse; she knew she'd be fine, didn't she?

"You aren't fine," he stated, almost reading her mind. "Are you stressed about the shooting? I'm still worried.?"

"I'm not a three-year-old," she snapped. "I'll be fine. I just need to rest." She doubled over, moaning. "Oh, the baby?" She didn't mean to blurt out her fear, it just came out.

"Oh, my god," Courtney blurted. "She rode like a madwoman to help Tommy. What if she hurt the baby?" She hurried across the small waiting room to April's side. "Seriously, April, you need to see a doctor. They need to do an ultrasound or something to check on the baby."

"Dammit, you should have taken it easy, you're pregnant," Wade complained.

"I'll thank you to mind your own business. Pregnant women ride all the time. It's fine. I'm fine." How could his concern both thrill and rankle her? She cried out under another wave of pain.

"But they don't ride that hard," Courtney corrected. "And you leapt off that horse like a demented woman." Courtney elbowed Wade. "Do something," she whispered.

"Is that true," Wade asked quietly, kneeling in front of April. "Did you ride too hard? I know riding is safe in the early stages, but you're in pain now, and it sounds like you went hell-bent-for-leather. Maybe you should have someone check on the baby."

"I'll be fine. The baby will be fine." Even she heard the wobble of doubt in her voice.

Wade looked at Courtney. "Go get a nurse." Obediently, Courtney hurried off and returned with a gray-haired nurse.

"I'm Evangeline," the woman stated. "This young woman tells me you're experiencing some difficulty."

"I'm a nurse. And I'm fine." April groaned as the pain slammed through her again.

"You're pregnant and, from what your friend says, you raced across several fields on a horse. You might have caused your baby some stress. Come on, let's get you looked at."

Waffling mentally, April sat frozen and undecided. The

medical practitioner in her said the cramps would pass, while the mother in her urged her to ensure her child was unharmed.

"Come on, April," Wade said, taking her hand. "Go with the nurse. Make sure the baby is okay. We're waiting on Tommy anyway." There was an edge of pleading in Wade's voice.

"Are you her husband?" Evangeline asked.

Wade shook his head, releasing her hand.

"The baby's father?"

"No, just a close friend."

The nurse studied the two of them. Her gaze finally settled on April. "Your friends are right. You really do need to see a doctor. Come with me."

"I can't. I'm scared," April whispered. "What if something is wrong?"

"Then all the better to get things checked out," Wade advised, gently tugging her to her feet. "Come on. Let's make sure that wee one is unharmed."

"Will you come with me?" she asked him, hating the shaking in her voice and legs.

"Me…" Wade blurted. "Why me? Why not Courtney? She's a woman."

"Please," April whispered. "I'm scared. You've been my knight in shining armor for days now. I need someone I can trust. I need you." She smiled apologetically at Courtney, who grinned back understandingly.

"Go on," Courtney urged. "I'll wait here for Tommy and you to come back." She settled into a chair and picked up a magazine.

Evangeline insisted April ride in a wheelchair for the short trip to the exam room. "Lucky for you, it's quiet. But then the Edson emergency room is rarely ever busy. Not much action here." She chatted on about the quiet life as a nurse in a small town.

Before April knew what was happening, she was standing beside an examination table with Wade outside the closed curtain. She slipped out of her clothing and into a hospital gown.

"Okay, I'm ready." She climbed up to sit on the bed, pulling the blanket over herself. Anxiety plagued her and she shivered, fear freezing out any rational thoughts.

"Goodness, you're shaking like a leaf." Evangeline came through the curtain opening. She disappeared again and returned with two warm blankets. She tucked one over April's legs and wrapped the other around her shoulders.

"All right. You can come in," she called toward the curtain.

Wade peeked his head in. "Still want me here?" he asked uncertainly. When April nodded, he strode quickly to her side and grasped her hand.

"Okay, you skipped triage, so we'll need to do some quick paperwork before the doctor arrives." Evangeline fired off some questions and April answered. Note taking complete, April lay back while the nurse performed a cursory, but thorough, examination. Still holding her hand, Wade turned politely away from April's exposed body.

"That's one heck of a scar," Evangeline commented. "How did you get that?"

"Knife wound. Occupational hazard. I was an ER nurse in the city."

"Drug addict or enraged patient?"

"He was a bit of both," April said.

"That's exactly why I left the Foothills Hospital in Calgary and moved out here to a small town. Too much drama for this old gal to handle. Besides, city driving was making me nuts." She laughed. "Okay, cover up. I'll send in the doctor."

The words were barely out of her mouth when the curtain slid back and a tall, balding man with an enormous smile and sparkling brown eyes strode through. "Hi, I'm Dr. Robins. I hear you're having some cramping after a crazy ride on a horse." He closed the curtain behind him. He repeated all the nurse's questions, seeking his own answers and probing for details.

"Do you want him here while I do an internal exam?" He nodded toward Wade, who had turned back around.

"God no," Wade blurted.

"Please," April begged. "Stay. Hold my hand. You can turn your back." She didn't understand her desperate need to have him there. Her panic and fear were annoying and discomfiting. She disliked childish, petulant patients, even when she understood their concerns. To see it in herself was mortifying.

Wade sighed and turned his back without releasing her hand. "As you wish."

"Evangeline is right," the doctor commented a few moments later. "That's one heck of a scar. Mind if I ask how many stitches?"

"One hundred eighty-six. Most of them on the surface. Just a few internal. No major damage. Just cosmetic. Suffice it to say, I don't wear a bikini anymore."

~

WADE TURNED HIS HEAD. He caught a glimpse of a large, slightly puckered, scar running diagonally across her body. Holy crap! That must have been one hell of an injury. His body hunched protectively. He could only see part of the scar. It disappeared up under the gown.

Realizing he was looking when he shouldn't be, he turned around again; but he couldn't erase the memory of that puckered scar on the smooth, round curve of her belly.

"Wow, it's huge. It must have hurt like hell. Will it give her trouble as she gets bigger?" he asked.

"You looked?" April asked, surprise in her voice.

Wade winced but didn't look at her. Dammit. He should learn to keep his mouth shut. "Sorry. I didn't mean to. But a hundred and eighty-six stitches? I couldn't help myself. Really, I looked without realizing it. I'm sorry. I won't look again. I promise."

"You're babbling." April laughed. "I'm rubbing off on you. Keep your eyes to yourself please, city-boy."

"I didn't see anything important," he claimed. God forbid that he'd seen any more of her. Just looking at the creamy expanse of her belly was distraction enough. God, he was a pervert, lusting after an injured woman. A pregnant one at that. But scar or no, that was the prettiest belly he'd seen in a while, even if there wasn't much to it, pregnancy had barely rounded her stomach.

"Listen to the patient," the doctor advised. "Or I'll have to ask you to leave. I'm going to do an internal now. But no, the scar shouldn't be an issue when April grows larger. It is fully healed. There might be some tightness, but it won't rupture or anything like that."

Wade heard the blankets shifting, rubber gloves snapping and April groaning lowly.

"Are you okay?" he asked. *Good grief.* This shouldn't be so difficult. He hardly knew the woman. He wasn't even sure why he was in this exam room with her; except that he couldn't seem to refuse her anything. If he didn't know better, he'd think he was falling for her. Good thing he knew better. Wade Kelly Borne did not fall for skinny women. Or needy women. Hell, he didn't fall for women. Marriage-seeking women and dishonest ex-fiancées were half of what drove him out of the city to start with.

"I'm fine," she responded with a grunt.

"Actually," the doctor corrected. "We're going to get an ultrasound done. You've got a bit of spotting and I want to check it out."

Gloves snapped, something hit the trash and the doctor said, "Okay, she's decent, you can turn around now. The tech will be back in with the equipment shortly."

"Spotting?" Wade asked, not understanding what the doctor meant.

"It means I'm having a bit of bleeding. Probably nothing. Some women spot all the way through their pregnancy." April's response was calm and easy.

"And you? Have you been spotting? I mean before this?"

April brought their clasped hands to her mouth and kissed his. "Relax, Prince Charming, the doctor didn't seem too upset."

"Isn't that his job? To be calm and to keep the patient calm? What if there is something wrong and he's not telling you? What about the baby?"

April chuckled. "Wade, relax. Chill. I'm a nurse. I know

how to read a doctor's voice, his instructions. This is strictly precautionary." She squeezed his hand tightly and sucked in a breath. "Okay, maybe there is a reason for the ultrasound, but I feel calmer now. Even if it's still uncomfortable." She patted his hand with her other hand.

"I'm supposed to be comforting you, not the other way around." He felt foolish and totally out of his element. Business was his forte, not women's issues. He knew nothing about pregnancy. Nothing. And here he was, helping a pregnant woman through a crisis and handling it like crap. God, he should have done a better job protecting her.

She'd even kissed him to make him feel better.

Whoa!

She'd kissed him!

He didn't know whether to cut and run or beg for more.

"See," April reassured him an hour later as they climbed into his truck. "It was nothing. Okay, not nothing, but the baby is fine. They gave me something to stop the cramping. Provided I stay off my feet for a few days, we'll both be fine."

"Why do I think it will be difficult to keep you in bed?" *Dammit, now I'm thinking of her in bed and those thoughts do not include resting. Shit. If I don't get myself together, I'll have to leave or risk getting in too deep, if I'm not already.*

"I intend to listen to the doctor's orders. This baby is the most important thing in my world. The ranch comes a distant second. I'll be able to rest and supervise things. Plus, there is always paperwork. Rest, bookkeeping and looking after my baby is my top priority. Nothing comes before her."

"Her? You know the baby is a girl?" Wade started the truck and backed out of the stall he'd hurried into earlier. *Won't that be lovely? A sweet baby girl with April's lovely, wheat-blonde hair and warm brown eyes.*

"No, they offered to tell me at my first trimester ultrasound, but I declined. I'm looking forward to the birth and the discovery of gender."

CHAPTER SEVENTEEN

They drove back to the ranch with Courtney and Tommy following in Courtney's car. Sergeant Miller was sending someone out to have a look around the ranch, but he wasn't optimistic they would find anything. That was the downfall of a ranch this size, a lot of ground to cover and plenty of places to hide. April's precious haven had turned into a dark place with horrors hiding behind every tree and rock.

The upside was that the doctor declared Tommy's wound a through and through, just as Courtney predicted. It had been a small caliber bullet, likely a .22 or a .223, and it hadn't done much damage. They had cleaned and dressed the wound. A couple of stitches and he was fit to return to the ranch. He'd be off his feet for a day or two, but he'd get the scar to go with his tale. He'd be keeping April company while they rested.

Jack met them in the kitchen and ladled out a late lunch of chicken stew and biscuits. "I went back to that dead cow. Coyotes were after her already, but I managed to get the tag and lasso the calf and fetch her home. If she survives, that'll be one more heifer to add to the breeding pool. We need to rebuild the herd. I put her in the corral with that calfless mother. Hopefully the cow will adopt the calf so we don't have to bottle feed."

"Bottle feeding would be awesome," Tommy piped up, between mouthfuls of food.

"Yeah, for the first few days," April agreed. "I did it as a kid. But calves eat continually and there's precious little rest for the feeder. You might as well sleep in the barn with an orphaned calf and count yourself lucky to get any rest. Besides, you're injured, so there's no way you're doing it."

"And we ain't got time for that foolishness," Jack proclaimed, pouring himself a coffee and settling on a chair. "We've got other issues."

April and Wade groaned in unison and then shared a look at the mirroring of thoughts.

"What is it now?" April asked tiredly.

"There are ATV tracks all over the place. Gates left open, cut fencing. I found several cows that ain't ours. Tag numbers don't match. I wrote them down and checked when I got back here. I put in a call to Livestock Identification Services. They're going to get back to us tomorrow. Seems there's an epidemic of stolen cattle in this area. So, it could be days before someone shows up to claim them."

"We'll need to round them up and separate them from the others," April mentioned with a groan. "That's going to be a ton of work. Thank heaven for cattle dogs."

"You're not riding," Courtney piped up. "Jeff, Jarrod and I have ridden before. We can help if Jack explains what to do.

There are enough horses, even if we leave out the two that were poisoned."

"That ain't a good idea," Jack blurted.

"It might be," April said thoughtfully. "That'll leave Wade here with the other four. Tommy and I will find something sedate to do. You'll have to watch them, Jack. And give them good directions, but other guests have helped in the past and these guys are eager to help. It won't be as fast as actual ranch hands, but at least you'll have company." She gestured vaguely for Jack's opinion.

He gave her a questioning look but didn't disagree. "Come on." He nodded toward his group. "Let's get this done. I'll explain as we go. We've got a couple hours of good daylight left."

They tromped out of the kitchen on his heels.

"A couple hours?" Wade questioned. "It doesn't get dark here until ten."

"True, but you can't work until full dark and it's been one heck of a long day already."

"You've got that right," Tommy laughed.

"Tommy, you and I will work in the office. I'll be right in, after I get everyone else set to a chore."

Tommy saluted and hobbled down the hall, leaning heavily on his crutches.

"I was thinking we could continue with the demolition, if that's acceptable?" Wade glanced questioningly at April.

"That isn't ranching," Ryan complained.

"Shut up, Ryan," Leticia, another of the students, warned him. "You're always bitching. About everything. It gets on my nerves."

"Technically, no, it isn't ranching," April intervened. "But tearing down a building and making repairs is critical. Admittedly, I'm not sure if the website you signed up on indicated what was going to happen during your stay, but when I was younger, Bale guests did exactly what the ranch hands did. Sometimes it involves animals and chores, other times less interesting work. When I was a kid, Bale guests built the raised garden beds. You spent the entire day with the animals yesterday. Tomorrow you'll be back there again. Of course, if you'd rather shovel out the barn…"

"I thought this would be more fun." He crossed his arms over his chest and frowned.

"I'm sorry it isn't what you expected," Wade commiserated. "But we can't be held accountable for your expectations. We have a system here at the Lazy-W. You can go with the flow, or you can leave. The choice is yours." He turned toward the remaining three. "Head out guys. You know where the tools are. I'll join you shortly. April and I have some ranch business to discuss."

Ryan followed behind the others, grumbling the entire way about how unfair it was that he didn't get to ride horses and play with kittens all day.

"Good gravy," April sighed. "The man's only been on a horse twice." She shook her head. "What did you want to discuss?"

"The kid's a spoiled punk. A week or two of hard work and real life will do him some good." He shrugged. "Well, the rest of them are game to work and learn. One bad apple in eight isn't too bad." He pulled out the chair beside April, spun it around and straddled it, facing her. He reached out and caressed her cheek with one finger.

"How are you, really?" He held her gaze with his. "The truth, please."

The truth? The truth was that she wanted to burst into tears and shout and throw things. She was angry and unsettled. But mostly, she was worried about her baby, the ranch's survival, and the unknown bastard who was threatening her livelihood and her future. She could still see the dead cow…

"Worried, upset, tired. But I think I'm going to be okay." He cupped her cheek with his hand and she leaned into it, closing her eyes for a second.

"Having you here helps. But I hate that I depend on you so much. You're supposed to be a guest here too." She laughed ironically. "Heck, you aren't supposed to be here at all. My fairy godmother must have been looking out for me when you showed up. You've been a godsend. I really appreciate everything you've done in the past four days."

"This wasn't what I set out to do on my sabbatical, but surprisingly, it's turning out to be the best vacation I've had in years. And I think that it's as much the company as the location. Although, I could use a day or two without excitement. What do you say that when things settle down, we take a long slow ride and have a picnic someplace?"

His request startled her. She stared at him in disbelief. What was he thinking? A date? No, that couldn't be, could it? He must mean just relaxing and unwinding without any accidents or gunfire. *Yeah, that's it!* She couldn't even formulate a response to the question; her thoughts scattered like dandelion seeds in the wind.

"Sorry," Wade eased his hand away from her face. "I didn't

mean to put you on the spot. Never mind. I'll just get back to work." He stood.

Grasping his hand, she tugged him gently back to his seat. "It's okay." Her face heated. "You just caught me off guard. If this string of catastrophes ever ends, I would love to take a ride and have a picnic with you. As friends." She watched his expression as she spoke. A frown turned to a half-smile and with the "friends" qualification morphed into disappointment.

Disappointment rolled around to fear for the future. Everything was topsy-turvy. Dead animals, strange tracks. For Pete's sake, Tommy had been shot. Her nerves were piano string tight. Something had to give or she'd snap in half. Her stomach churned and her shoulders ached. She couldn't bear to think about something else going wrong, or someone being hurt. She wanted to cry. She closed her eyes to keep tears from leaking out.

"I don't know what to do," April whispered. "I can barely handle the ranch. All these problems are piling up and I don't know how I'm going to cope. I don't even know where to begin with day to day chores. Dealing with the crazy stuff going on is making me nuts."

To her dismay, she burst into tears.

DAMN. He hated when women cried. Her sobs were a knife to Wade's guts. He didn't blame April, she'd been through hell since he arrived, and long before that. He slid his chair around the table to sit beside her, he drew her into his arms.

"Hey, it's okay. We'll work this out." He had no freaking

idea how, but he had to do something. Her tears and her strength were tearing him apart. She needed him. Strangely, he didn't mind, too much, though he hated women who cried to get their way. This was different, she wasn't manipulating him, she was the strongest woman he'd ever met. She'd been attempting to handle these disasters on her own, with no help from him. He admired that. He massaged her shoulders, wishing he could do more. After a moment, she straightened up.

"I'm okay now." She sniffed, pulled a tissue from her pocket and wiped her eyes.

He hadn't expected asking her on a picnic would trigger a waterfall.

"Listen, I didn't mean any pressure. I meant—oh hell, I don't know what I meant." Damn. He'd frightened her without even knowing he was asking for a date. Why was he asking for a date? It didn't make sense. He'd fled from the city to get away from women and now he was trying to get closer to one. A skinny, pregnant woman with a ranch full of issues, at that. This sabbatical was supposed to be about relaxing and escaping problems and here he'd gone and landed smack dab in the middle of a pile of manure with exactly the type of woman he was trying to avoid.

So why wasn't he running, screaming, to his truck and spraying gravel as he hit the road? Ha. That one was easy. With the dead cow, the dead bull, the shooting and all the broken fencing, there was no way he'd leave a pregnant woman virtually alone to deal with it all. He had to be sure she was safely back on her feet with nothing left to fear, so he'd get back to work. He rose and stepped back from the table.

"April? Are you in here?" A female voice called from the front door.

"Beth?" April called out.

The door opened and banged gently shut. "In the flesh. I just got back from town. I heard you were at the hospital?" A short, pudgy, redhead rounded the corner into the kitchen. She stopped dead in the doorway. "And who might this tall drink of water be? Have you been hiding him from me?"

"Beth Wood, meet Wade Kelly. He's a paying guest for a few days. Wade, this is Beth, my neighbor and friend. She's a sweetheart but a colossal pain in the arse."

"Wade Kelly?" Beth questioned. "Why do you look familiar? Do I know you? Have we met? Why are you here?" She looked back and forth between April and Wade, questions in her eyes.

"Sorry, I don't think we've met. And I have no idea why I might seem familiar." Good gravy, don't let the woman realize who he was and blab it to April. That would ruin his entire vacation and any chance he might have of dating her.

Whoa! Where had that come from? Every time he turned around; he was thinking of April romantically. This was not good. No, this was bad. Very, very bad. These thoughts had to end. Now!

"But I'm pleased to meet you." He offered his hand.

They shook and Beth studied him with a slight squint that had him squirming and wanting to confess all his sins. Back in high school, he'd called that look the teacher stare.

She dropped his hand and whirled round to look at April. "So, what's up, buttercup? Why were you in the hospital? This dude looks fine. I saw Jack and he's fine. That leaves you..." she trailed off expectantly.

"I wasn't at the hospital for me. Well, I was, but that isn't why I went there," April babbled.

"Sure, that clears it right up." Beth slid into a chair opposite to April. "Spill it, girl."

"Where's Herb?"

"Out counting his chickens." She waved dismissively. "Never mind trying to deflect me with my husband. Dish…"

"Dish?" April laughed. "How antiquated. Okay, one of our guests got shot."

Beth grabbed her chest and gasped. "What?"

"So," Beth said, when the story wound to conclusion. "You neglected to tell me you are pregnant, that you have guests and that this stud is living with you? Did I miss anything?"

Wade choked back a laugh. This woman didn't miss a trick and had a phenomenal gift for dealing the guilt card. A woman like Beth would go far in business. He leaned against the doorway and waited. This would be good.

April looked down and blushed. "Sorry, Beth. I wasn't ready to share that information. You know all about Stan. I'm still in a daze after that fiasco and the debacle at work. I'm trying to find level ground to rest on, but it hasn't been easy. I've been so busy I haven't even had time to call you. I swear I'll do better. And he isn't living with me, he's just sleeping in the house for protection."

Beth chuckled. "That's one handsome bodyguard you have there."

Heat rose in Wade's face and he stared at his socks.

"Give me a hug, girl. You need one," Beth demanded gently. They stood and embraced.

Wade smiled at the pair. Beth was short and round against

April's tall and slender. What a duo! He was inordinately pleased to discover she had more people in her support group.

When they stepped apart, he spoke. "I'm off to supervise demolition. We'll be back in time to cook a late supper. Stay off your feet and rest, please. Nice meeting you, Beth." He waved and headed for the porch.

He wasn't even off the porch when he heard Beth's voice. "Wowsers!"

Feeling only slightly guilty, he stopped to listen.

"That is one hot man. And he seems familiar somehow. Like I should know him or I've seen his face or something."

"He's okay."

"Okay," Beth laughed. "He's gorgeous. I wish I was single. I'd like a taste of that one."

Wade choked back a laugh. Beth was a hoot. But he suspected that if she figured out who he was, she'd squeal on him in a heartbeat. He'd have to keep his guard up when she was around.

"He's been very nice to me. He's been a lot of help around here," April explained. "And yah, he's kind of cute. Too bad he's only a guest…"

And that was his cue to leave them to their visit. He'd eavesdropped enough for one day.

CHAPTER EIGHTEEN

The next morning, everyone was milling around outside the barn waiting for Beth and her husband, Herb, to arrive. As if enough hadn't changed on the Lazy-W already, Herb was bringing over some new livestock. This time it wasn't cows or horses.

"A pig?" Courtney asked? "Really?"

"A pregnant sow, to be precise. And a mama and baby goat. Some chicks and a rabbit hutch."

"Why?" Tommy sat on the seat of the quad, which they'd driven him to the lower yard on. "Why are they bringing them over?" he asked.

"Herb and Beth and I knew each other when I was a kid. Later, Beth used to work here when the bed and breakfast was open. Grampa Morgan did them a few favors when Herb inherited their ranch and they were just starting out. They're just returning the favor. It's how things work out here."

"That's so cool," Tommy said. "I like the help-out attitude. Like paying it forward by paying for the coffee for the guy behind you in the drive-thru. I could get used to living like that. I'm kind of surprised, actually. I didn't think I'd like it here, but I came because everyone else was coming. I thought I'd miss the city. But I like the peace and quiet."

"Me too," Wade chimed in. "I could get used to this if I had half a chance."

"Oh, here they come," April exclaimed, noticing the pristine white pickup coming slowly up the roadway, Herb and Beth inside.

Herb backed the truck into the spot April waved to and Beth jumped out to hug her tightly. "I'm so excited to do this for you. I'm glad we can pay back the help your grandfather gave us. Everyone, this is my husband, Herb." She gestured toward a tall, gangly man as he stepped out of the truck.

Herb tipped his cowboy hat with a blush and moved to open the stock trailer attached to the back of the three-quarter ton Ford.

"He's shy. Give him a while to get to know you and he'll chatter your ears off," Beth advised.

Everyone stood back and watched as Beth and Herb off-loaded a lumbering sow into a heavy wire mesh pen reinforced with steel poles. Inside the pen, a sterilized and recycled oil tank had been cut in half and flipped on its side and modified slightly to provide housing for the sow and her expected piglets. Long since out of use, the pen had a mud pit and watering trough. The fences remained sound and it was full of tall wild grass that would supplement the sow's feed as well.

What a blessing that the pigpen and goat field were still intact. Jack had double checked them last night, after talking to April about Beth's plan to help them restock their animals.

These animals were an enormous gift and she was grateful for them. And for Wade, who pulled his weight and more.

The two goats, on leashes, were led to a tightly fenced pen with man-made hills and humps and several climbing structures.

"That looks like a playground," Ryan exclaimed.

"It is. Goats love to climb and play. Notice how the fences aren't climbable and all the structures are far from the edges? Goats are masterful escape artists. But they're fun to play with, guests like them and goat milk cheese is divine," April gushed.

They watched the goats explore their new habitat while Herb unhitched the trailer.

Everyone pitched in to unload the heavy rabbit hutch and settle it up against the side of the chicken coop. They'd fasten it to the wall later, to ensure it didn't get tipped over accidentally.

"No rabbits?" Courtney asked.

"Late next week we've got a couple litters due to leave the doe, the mother. We'll bring them over then. Now, for the cutest things ever…" She returned to the truck and brought back a box of chicks. "We haven't checked them for gender yet. We haven't had time. We'll leave that to you." She handed out some chicks for everyone to hold.

"You'll need to keep them warm and near their food and water. Spread some pine shavings, we brought some, on the floor of the coop and cover it with newspapers. Then keep the floor scattered with chick feed. We brought some of that too, and keep the food and water troughs full. They'll grow fast. When they're bigger, you can ditch the paper and shavings. Before long, you'll have fresh eggs for brekky."

Everyone made a fuss over the chicks and chatted excitedly over the prospect of baby bunnies. Eventually, they got the chicks settled into the coop across the driveway from the barn, close to the goats. The yard was set up with large animals and the rabbit hutch on one side and small ones on the other, alongside parking for equipment.

"Do they know you'll be eating the rabbits?" Beth asked.

"Good lord, don't tell them that. These are city slickers. Some of them would lose their minds." April laughed. "And I'm not mentioning the chicken on the menu. It's crazy how many people have no idea where meat comes from."

With all the critters settled into their new homes, everyone regrouped at the house for coffee and the cookies Ryan and Leticia had baked as part of their morning kitchen duties. There was a lot of conversation about farm life and things in general.

April glanced up from her conversation with Herb to discover Beth, Jack and Wade whispering in the corner of the kitchen. She wandered over.

"What's up?" she asked, looking from one to the other.

"Nothing," Jack growled. He pivoted on his heel and left.

"Just having a difference of opinion, nothing serious," Beth exclaimed.

"Nope, nothing to see here." Wade laughed a little too brightly.

The tension in his shoulders belied his calm attitude. Something was up between the three of them and April doubted it was just a difference of opinion. She pinned the two remaining offenders, one after the other, with a glare. "Seriously? What's going on?"

Beth and Wade shared a look.

"I think he's letting you work too hard." Beth shrugged and tucked her hands into her pockets.

"I said I'm letting you set the pace. This isn't my ranch, nor is it my place to tell you how to take care of that baby. We differ on how much work is acceptable, that's all." He glanced away.

She studied the duo again. Yeah, they were lying, she'd bet her eye teeth on it. But whatever they were lying about, she doubted they'd let her in on the real reason for the argument. "You're lying. Both of you," she accused. "I expect you'll explain it to me eventually."

She pivoted on her heel and walked away. Letting them get away with their deception might have been the hardest thing she'd ever done. She was a stickler for honesty and she knew Wade was keeping secrets from the start. Now it seemed that Beth was in on it. That was both irksome and comforting. If it was something heinous, Beth would tell her, so whatever they were in cahoots about couldn't be too serious, even if her friend seemed to be agreeing only reluctantly. She was counting on Wade's promise not to lie to her.

What were they hiding? The question plagued her all day and well into the next. The only thing she was certain of was that time had a way of revealing all secrets.

CHAPTER NINETEEN

Two days later, April was up and about and Tommy was back to work. Tommy had the expected residual pain and had to be careful not to tear out his stiches and April planned to take it easy. She wasn't about to risk her baby's health. She was hoping some of the kids would stay on for an extra week. The extra help was nice and she was enjoying their company. This was their fifth day and they were scheduled for seven. Back in Grampa Morgan's day, Bale guests often extended their stays for weeks or months. One student had stayed six months before hiring on as a ranch hand, not leaving until Uncle John had taken over.

But increased guests were still a dream. Still, she cast a quick wish heavenward, hoping someone chose to stay. Perhaps they'd even get some guests signing up on the new website, now that the old one was down. The police wouldn't say who'd set up the original site. They repeatedly claimed the investigation was ongoing. Tommy had used his downtime well. He'd arranged a discount on Internet service through his brother and had set up a new website and e-mail for the Lazy-

W. They'd taken Wade's advice regarding pricing and conditions for staying at the ranch. His lawyer and friend, Rex Tremble, was due today to talk about sorting out the ranch affairs. He was also bringing some liability contracts for future guests to sign.

"April? Are you in here?" Wade called from the front of the house. "Rex is here."

"In the office." *Well, here goes nothing.* Hope rushed through her. Maybe they'd find a way out of this debacle. She pondered how much explaining she'd have to do. She wasn't certain what details Wade had provided the lawyer. Wade and Rex joined her in the office. Rex was in his mid-fifties, tall and well dressed. He had a ready smile and a calm manner.

"So, Miss Cooper. Mr. Kelly tells me that you need some work done. Pro-bono," he added gently. "Lucky for you, I have an open spot. My pro-bono tends to be full." He glanced at Wade and they shared a look.

What did that look mean? What was up between these two? It seemed like Wade was always sharing significant looks with others. Mistrust rocked through her. If he was lying…

"Thanks for coming." She shook Rex's hand. "Here's the situation. My grandfather died. His Will is missing, but last time I saw it, the will stated the Lazy-W was to go equally to my father and my uncle John. Days after Grampa Morgan passed, my father died in an unexplainable car accident. Dad bequeathed all his possessions to me, not that he had anything. All I received was a bill for his funeral. He didn't own anything but a broken-down car. It's crazy. Grampa got sick, Dad died, Uncle John ran the ranch into the ground and now he's missing. People are shooting at us. Poisoning, killing or stealing our livestock and all sorts of crazy things are happening. The bank won't let me access the accounts, although statements tell me the money is all gone. I want to get this place back up on its feet, but the bank is coming after me for outstanding loans. I have no money. I have no job. Frankly, I'm lost. Grampa Morgan had a life insurance policy, I think, but I don't know if it was ever paid out. Barely anyone will talk to me as I'm not the executor of his Will. That was Uncle John, if I remember correctly. It just goes around and around in circles and I'm lost." Finally spent, her words ground to a halt. *Good lord, I was babbling again. When will I learn not to spill my guts?*

Rex made a few notes as she talked. He set his pen down. "Okay. As I see it, the first order of business is to get the court to grant you temporary control over the ranch while everything is being sorted out." He jotted a few more notes on the legal pad. "Next, we investigate the insurance and talk to the bank about holding off on the debt for a few more months, hopefully until we get this straightened out. They won't stop charging interest, but I've often convinced banks to let the payments slide in unusual circumstances like this. Of course, the debt rises and, in the end, if we fail at everything, they'll get a bigger chunk of the ranch in compensation."

"What?" Dismay washed over her.

"It's not as bad as it sounds," Wade advised. "Rex has done a lot of this. We'll find you a way out of this mess."

His smile was reassuring. They carried on discussing options and formulating a plan. Then they went over the new guest contracts, drawn up by a lawyer in Rex's office, and April approved them on Wade's assurance they were okay.

"Now, one last thing," Rex said brightly. "I've managed to secure you a donation from a benefactor I know. He specializes in helping struggling small businesses. It's a charitable organization that he uses, in part, for a tax shelter. It is an influx of cash, albeit a small one, but it does come with one caveat. You must agree to never search out the benefactor, nor shall you mention this to anyone else. He wishes to remain anonymous in all his donations."

"Why?" April demanded, not liking the sound of the restriction. It smacked of secrecy and made her nervous.

"Because he doesn't like publicity," Rex informed her. "He wants to remain private. His instruction is that if you accept the donation, you'll find a way to pay it forward when you get back on your feet. If that doesn't happen, heaven forbid, his advisors will consider adjusting the requirements for the future recipients. It will be my responsibility to keep him informed of the status of the ranch and how the funds are used."

"Wade? What do you think?" she asked, without thinking. She was relying on him more than she should. She wanted to resurrect the Lazy-W by her own merits, and here she was using Wade and his connections. It didn't sit right.

Wade hesitated a few seconds. "Well, if it is a tax shelter for the guy and you've met his requirements, I don't see the harm. There doesn't seem to be a need to repay the donation if this doesn't work out. And I'm not saying it won't." He turned to Rex. "You do this on a regular basis for this client?"

"This benefactor makes these donations semi-regularly. Usually on the recommendation of the charity's board of directors. I've worked with him for years. This time, I brought your situation to him, because you did appear to fit his requirements. And now, after talking to you and getting Mr. Kelly's input, I think you're a good fit for the program. The benefactor's main interest is helping worthy small businesses stay afloat. Occasionally, the donation comes with a clause that requires the owner to take some extra training but, in this case, that doesn't apply." He smiled at April and mentioned a sum.

"He wants to give me that much?" Her voice rose in alarm. "I can't take that much. I could buy a luxury car with that."

"Yes, you could," Wade agreed. "Although, that might not be the best use of the money." He chuckled. "But you could do some repairs and maybe hire a hand until you're back on your feet after the baby comes."

"Oh, my gosh. That's so amazing." She leapt up and hugged Rex and then Wade, kissing him on the cheek. "Thank you. Thank you. Thank you. This is incredible."

"Hang on, missy," Rex laughed. "We have to get the bank to back down and open new accounts first. It could take a couple weeks, but the money is coming. If I fail to get the bank to back down, and I never have, we'll have to reconsider our options."

April hugged herself. Even those words, that caveat, didn't dampen her enthusiasm. "I can do this," she whispered. "I can actually make this a home for me and my baby. Thank you so much."

"Now," Rex continued, "I'd like to recommend a firm to help you hire a new hand, if that's your intention. They've agreed to do this pro-bono, although they usually charge. Your benefactor recommended them and I often use them myself. Waterson Ripley Reece is a head-hunting firm. They don't typically do ranch hiring, but they are game to try and they've never failed me. If you decide to hire a hand, you can't do so before you receive the funds, but we should start the ball in motion. Unless you know someone you trust enough to hire."

That was a whole different ball of twine. So many men had been employed over the years. Some would be too old; many would have found other jobs. Heck, some of them were probably out of work. But who had worked for Uncle John? He'd run the ranch into a wreck. Could anyone who worked for him be trusted? All the personnel files were missing, so there was no help there.

"I'll ask around. Maybe one of the neighbors know of someone. Times are tough and I'm sure they've had to let people go. But please start the search. I would like to hire someone as soon as I can. Wade can't stay on as a guest and ad-hoc foreman forever. He has his own life and his own business."

The idea of Wade leaving made her stomach clench. She liked having him around. Not only because he was helping her out, but also because he was kind, generous and good company. She was learning so much about business from him. Mostly, she'd miss his smile. What she wouldn't miss was the unending urge to touch him or kiss him. Nope, those urges she wouldn't miss, but she'd sure know he was gone.

A soft sigh escaped. This past week had been crazy. So many ups and downs. The highs and lows were driving her crazy. She was starting to feel like she was spiraling out of control. There wasn't enough time between the emotional peaks and dips to recalibrate and regain her equilibrium. This stress couldn't be good for the baby.

"Are you all right?" Wade guided her back to her chair.

"I'm good. Sort of. The ups and downs are taking their

toll," she confessed, hating herself for doing so. "I need to relax. I used to meditate when I was a kid and my dad was being nuts." *Oh great, another confession.* "I think I need to try again, to see if I can calm down and re-center." *Now I sound like some woo-woo hippy. I really needed to get a grip.* Another sigh slipped out.

"Perhaps you're overtired," Rex suggested.

"Why don't you go lie down for a while?" Wade agreed. "A nap might help. I had a pregnant secretary once. She napped every afternoon. She asked to come in early and go home later to compensate. It was what worked for her, so I agreed and I shortened her hours a bit. I'm no fool. A happy employee works hard and she's been the best assistant I'd ever had. Come on, April, let me help you upstairs so you can nap."

"I'm pregnant, not an invalid. I can find my own way upstairs. Thanks for all the help, Mr. Tremble. I really do appreciate it." She offered her hand.

"Lovely to meet you. I can see why Mr. Kelly called me. You're a nice woman in need of a helping hand. I'm honored to be able to assist. I'll have him show me out, if that's okay. Please go rest and I'll get back to you as soon as I can."

"Thank you." She smiled tiredly and left the office.

She didn't make it as far as the stairs. She chose instead to nap on Grampa Morgan's bed in the master bedroom on the main floor. Stairs seemed like too much of an effort. She'd barely laid down when she was asleep.

"THANKS FOR KEEPING my name out of this." Wade smiled.

"She'd kick up one hell of a stink if she knew I was her benefactor."

"She sure would. I can tell she's got a stubborn, independent streak. I think she'll make a go of this place if we can remove those major hurdles for her. What I don't understand is why you're here and not at the office. And look at those clothes. You look like an old farmer who grew six inches and shed fifty pounds overnight." He laughed.

"Grampa Morgan's clothes. I haven't gone to town and get my own. I can't wear suits and leather shoes for ranch work."

"Why *are* you here?" Rex repeated.

"Damned if I know. I found her in a broken-down truck on the side of the road and gave her a ride home. She offered coffee as thanks. The bull was shot before I left and things just escalated out of control. The strangest thing is that I don't want to leave. I've got a multi-billion-dollar company to run and I'll be damned if I care."

"Son, I told you, months ago, you were burning out and that you had to step away. You should have listened." He shook his head in a way that made Wade feel like a chastised teenager.

"I did. That's why I ran into April out here in the back of beyond. I grabbed a bag, jumped in my truck and took off. No set destination, just away from the office, from Barbara and her lies and the crazy herds of women chasing me for my money." He flopped into a chair and sighed. "I'm doing double duty, relaxing and looking for a place to purchase for a corporate retreat. This place would have been perfect...before I got to know April."

"What happened between you and Barbara? You ended that engagement in quick order. I didn't even know there was trouble until you called to have me rescind her credit cards and get your car back."

"She was sleeping with someone else. In my bed, in my apartment. I'd have left her anyway, but my bed? My house? Can you believe I actually thought she loved me? I'm a damned fool." He rubbed his forehead with his fingertips.

"And here you are, giving handouts to another woman. Are you sure this is what you want to do?" Rex's voice was gently chiding and commiserating all at once.

"Do you have the report I asked for?" He changed the subject.

"She seems on the up and up. I didn't find much. No unpaid parking tickets, no debt. She was engaged but that's been over for a while. You knew that."

"What aren't you telling me? I can hear it in your voice." He braced himself. If Rex didn't want to tell him, it must be something big, a deal-breaker. But if it was a deal-breaker, why hadn't he mentioned it outside, before they talked to April?

"She was accused of drug theft and subsequently fired from her job as an ER nurse in Calgary," Rex advised him in his typical no-nonsense fashion.

"What? Why didn't you tell me?" Anger clogged his throat. His fists bunched.

"I did some further investigation, or rather had it done. Seems she's was never accused or convicted of any other crime. She was not arrested or charged in the drug thefts, just dismissed with a notation made in her file. The thefts came as a shock to everyone she worked with. Nobody believed her capable of the thefts, or of drug use. Several of her closest coworkers claim it was her ex who had the drug problem and that April was unaware of it. The ex, I might add, is currently cohabitating with April's former superior, the woman who instigated her firing. They've got it all tied up in a neat bow and I don't like it one bit."

Several conflicting opinions ran through Wade's mind before he settled on a decision. "Okay, put another man on it. Find out the truth. I tend to agree she doesn't seem the drug type. She didn't even have any over-the-counter pain meds in the house. We had to pick them up for Tommy after he was shot."

"There's more," Rex advised.

"What now?" Exasperation made his voice tense.

"I don't think the uncle is dead. No proof, mind you, just some rumors. I've got some feelers out regarding the uncle. There are too damn many coincidences here."

"What kind of feelers?"

"Do you really want to know?"

"Never mind. I know you have contacts from less desirable aspects of society. They've served us well in the past. But honestly, do you think she's a good risk? I admit my attraction to her might be skewing my judgment."

"I hear the questions, the concern, in your voice. You always could hide it from everyone but me and your folks. If I didn't think she was worth the risk, I'd have told you so right off the bat. And if it turns out I'm wrong, the money you're giving her is small potatoes and the tax deduction worth it."

They chatted quietly for about an hour before Rex hit him with a whopper of a question. "So, when are you coming back? *Are* you coming back? If not, what are you planning?"

"Frankly, I don't know. I've lost my passion for business. I feel like I should step down. Maybe turn the reigns over to

Bronson. He's been my number one man for years. Now that I'm out here, living a simpler life, I think it's time to retire."

Rex laughed at that statement. "You'll never retire. But there are other options."

"Such as?"

"Answer me this first. Are you enthralled with the quiet or the woman?"

Tough question. The answer was simple and complex. Both had their appeal, though frankly, there had been precious little peace to go with that quiet. This ranch was a madhouse of problems stacked on atop the other, he spent half his time wondering what disaster would swamp them next. He loved the ranch life. While he'd only been here for a few days, it brought back memories of his childhood. He'd always been a quick decision maker and had never stumbled over decisions or lamented mistakes, except Barbara, or Barbie, as she preferred to be called. He felt like now was the time to step down. That dissatisfaction, combined with his ex, had instigated the sabbatical. But what about April? Was she influencing his decision? He couldn't honestly say one way or the other.

"Honestly, it's part April, and part the different pace. Additionally, I think—correction—I know, it's time to step back. Perhaps not let go of the reigns completely. But I need to let go. I've lost the joy in the job. Money doesn't buy happiness you know."

"That's rich, coming from you," Rex replied with the candor that only respected colleagues could get away with. "There are options..."

"Such as?" Wade repeated his earlier question.

"You can live anywhere and take a lesser role in your

companies. Find yourself a place in a small town, or in the country. Hell, live here for all I care. I just know you aren't ready to retire, but you do need a break. You could give Randolph the money-making end. Let him run that. Take over the charitable side yourself. Consider it. Think outside the box. That's how you got as far as you did. And dear God, tell her who you are before she finds out on her own."

CHAPTER TWENTY

The sound of arguing woke April from a sound sleep. Disorientation rocked her until she realized she was still in her grandfather's bed. Listening for a moment, she heard three voices. Wade, a woman and another man. Rising, she finger-combed her hair, straightened her clothing and headed for the kerfuffle.

"Do you mind telling me what this is all about?" She asked, stepping out onto the front porch. The screen door banged shut behind her. The man who'd made the laughable offer on her land the other day, stood beside a tall, scrawny blonde woman with generously enhanced cleavage. She wore shoes that cost more than April made in a year as a nurse. Her dress was short and tight and her hair was quaffed into within an inch of its life. A hurricane wouldn't shake that do. She could be a model, or a hooker.

"You? Again?" April stared at the developer's agent, Kurt Werner. "I told you I wasn't interested in selling the ranch."

"April, sorry to wake you." Wade moved over to stand beside her. "They were just leaving."

"I came back to alter the offer." He stood there with a smug I'm-going-to-show-you look, his hand resting on the arm of the woman beside him. He mentioned an offer that was a third higher than the ridiculously low offer he'd made before. Initially, she'd considered the offer generous, but Wade had enlightened her as to why it was a low-ball joke.

"I'm not interested. Please go." Certain that this conversation was pointless, she turned to head back inside.

"I suggest you take this offer. You might not have another chance," Werner mocked. "Triad Resorts doesn't often make a second offer."

Triad Resorts was huge, they had properties all over the world. It was odd that they'd be interested in a run-down ranch in Alberta. "What do they want with this land?" she demanded. She glanced at Wade, noting his angry scowl. Was it related to Werner's mention of Triad? Did he know something? She was about to ask him when the blonde spoke up.

"Do you know who he is?" She smiled coldly.

"Yes." April turned back toward them. "Kurt Wiener, oh sorry, Kurt Werner. Peon for Triad Resorts."

"Not him. Him." She stabbed a dagger-like finger with a blood red nail toward Wade. "Do you know who he really is? Have you any idea who you're screwing?"

"Number one, I'm not screwing anyone. Number two, I do know who he was. Number three, get off my land before I call the police." *Good gravy, why am I even acknowledging the questions, let alone answering them?* She was losing her grip and was exhausted from the crap the universe kept piling onto her.

The blonde tipped her head, raising her chin disdainfully.

"That man is my ex-fiancé. He's a multi-billionaire business tycoon. I have no reason why he's out here in the sticks slumming it."

"I am well aware that Wade is a businessman. He's also my guest. As for being your ex, it's clear to see why he dumped you. Thank you for that non-information. Have a good day. I'm calling the police now. If either of you set foot on my property again, I'll have you arrested for trespassing. And you can tell Triad to stuff their offer where the sun doesn't shine." She pivoted and entered the house, slamming the screen door behind her for emphasis.

She stormed down the hallway to the kitchen. Wine, she needed wine. She paused in the threshold. Not wine, the baby couldn't have wine. But dammit, she needed something. Coffee. Slamming cupboards and drawers to drown out the heated conversation on the porch, she started a pot of coffee and then assembled the ingredients for cookies.

Hell yes, she needed comfort food. About six dozen cookies and a pint of ice cream should do it.

"Are you okay?" Wade asked quietly from the door.

"What do you think?" she snarled, not turning to look at him. God, he had his nerve. A multi-millionaire and she was working him like a dog. She wanted to sink into the floor and disappear.

"It wasn't my intention to lie to you," he offered quietly.

She whirled around, hurling a bag of raisins at his head. He caught it deftly and her anger spiked. "Just when exactly were you planning to tell me?"

"You know I'm a businessman. I told you that. I told you I had an ex."

The words fell flat. The momentary silence following his

statement was deafening. Her heart thundered in her ears; her knees wobbled.

"A multi-millionaire?" She quipped. "That's a far cry from a businessman. What exactly is your business, Wade Kelly?" Like a lightning bolt, it hit her. She knew who he was and why he'd seemed vaguely familiar.

"Wade Kelly? Wade Kelly Borne? WKB Well-Servicing? Are you freaking kidding me?" She stumbled to a chair and dropped into it. "I've been playing hostess and ordering around the province's richest man? Treating him like a dog's-body? Good lord. Why didn't you tell me?" She was seriously sick to her stomach. Even cookies lost their appeal. All she wanted was him off her land and long gone. She'd deal with the damage to her heart and self-worth later.

"Why should I? I enjoyed being treated like an ordinary person, not like a check book. You never ordered me, or anyone else around. You treat everyone with kindness and respect. It was a treat to work here and help you out. This is my vacation. Not knowing who I was wasn't hurting you."

It all started making sense. The look on Riley Wilson's face when he phoned the bank about Wade's credit card and how Wade cut him off before he could use a last name. Riley's sudden agreeability. How everyone, including the RCMP, seemed to know him. The argument between Wade, Jack and Beth. She'd been duped by them all.

She'd been caught peeing on the side of the road by a quad-zillionaire. Great.

She groaned. Now there was the perfect injury to add to the insult. It was like a tabloid headline, "*GQ* Candidate Catches Destitute Pregnant Rancher Peeing at the Roadside."

"And the lawyer? I suppose you're paying him too? And

my benefactor? That's you? I won't take your stupid money." She slammed a bag of sugar on the counter, busting it open. Her voice dropped to a whisper. "Was anything you told me true? Anything at all?"

"Everything. I am Wade Kelly. I just omitted my last name. I am on vacation. Barbara was my fiancée. Rex is my lawyer and he is working for you, pro-bono. It's a new program at my company. My lawyers do a set number of hours per week of charity work. And yes, I am your benefactor. I have a small charity that makes donations to small businesses. There's an application process. You can be recommended or apply. I just skipped that part."

"And would I have qualified, if I had applied?" She knew the answer.

"Probably not," he admitted. "But, it's my charity, and I can override the selection committee anytime I want. I like what I see here. I like the opportunity you give others for a country vacation, like the ones I had as a kid. The Bale concept is a sound business strategy. It's obvious you know ranching and are willing and eager to learn more about business management, hiring and finances. You have everything it takes to succeed in business. The only issue is with the messed-up ownership and what your uncle has done."

"Is there even a kernel of truth in that statement? Which part of that is the lie? All of it? A lie of omission is still a lie. I think you should pack your shit and leave. I'll refund your money as soon as I can. Feel free to start accruing interest, as of now. And you can take your donation and stuff it up your ass. Be gone when I get back."

CHAPTER TWENTY-ONE

*A*pril stormed out the kitchen door, slid into some rubber boots and then stomped down the boardwalk before marching off into the trees. She rushed through the bush, following a rough path, barely more than a game trail until a stitch in her side forced her to slow down.

What a fool she'd been. Ignoring her instincts that he seemed familiar. Trusting another man. Hadn't she vowed to stop trusting men after the fiasco with Stan? Men were jerks. Every last man-jack of them. Her uncle ruined the ranch and its legacy. Her father travelled from place to place living like a pauper, settling with any random woman who would support him. Her ex, Stan, lied, cheated, used drugs and stole from her and the hospital. Wade lied about who he was. When would the cycle of lies end? When would she wake up and smell the coffee?

Coffee?

Dammit, she'd stormed off without her coffee. Her anger at herself doubled. She couldn't even do that right. She'd left the cookie mess on the counter, sugar all over the counter and floor. Great. She could look forward to cleaning that up. If it wasn't one damn thing, it was sixteen others. Crap piled on crap.

She climbed over a section of wooden fence and trudged on. Her anger was fading to disillusion with every step. She had to get beyond this. She had to turn the ranch around and make it a success. Or maybe she should just sell it and move to Saskatchewan, where nobody had ever heard of April Cooper and the Lazy-W.

Damn. She couldn't even sell it with everything up in the air like it was. Should they ever figure out who owned it, the bank had dibs on a huge portion of the proceeds. Her heart wouldn't even consider letting someone else live in the only happy place she'd known in her childhood. It just got worse and worse. How many bombshells was she supposed to absorb without blowing into splinters of emotion.

Clouds skittered in front of the sun, turning the warm day chilly. Crows cried in the distance and a coyote barked. She turned her eyes to the sky. Whatever the crows were after wasn't far. She scurried in that direction. It could be anything. A natural death, a predator's kill, a still-birth, an injured cow. The rancher inside her demanded she investigate, no matter how fractured her heart was.

She pushed her way through thick underbrush into a clearing, her arrival chasing off the crows. They scattered with squawks of warning to the far side of the clearing, temporarily abandoning their feast.

She hurried toward the small furry body, tears welling in her eyes. That body looked familiar. It looked a lot like one of her dogs.

No!

She dropped to her knees beside the body and gathered it into her arms, heedless of the blood staining her clothing and dripping off her hands. A small hole, a bullet hole, pierced the dog's side. "Oh, Biscuit," she crooned at the undersized Australian Shepherd in her arms." She knelt there, rocking back and forth, tears dripping onto Biscuit's fur. This was the last fucking straw. She was going to find out who did this and rip them to shreds.

Biscuit had been born just after Grampa Morgan's death. April had helped deliver the pup when she was home for her grandfather's funeral. Biscuit had always been her favorite cattle dog. Jack had explained how, with too many genetic flaws to be a good breeder, she'd been spayed as a pup. Uncle John had wanted her put down, but Jack had adopted her as his, and even John hadn't dared interfere. Even on three legs, Biscuit had been a good cow dog, running and herding with the best of them.

When April came home, Biscuit had ditched Jack in favor of her new mistress, April. Jack had groused a lot but hadn't really minded. The duo had become fast friends.

Murder was no way for anyone to leave the world. Especially not April's favorite canine companion.

The loss of the dog she'd known from the day Biscuit was born cut deeply. They'd been virtually inseparable since she returned. She'd cried a million tears into her friend's fur, lamenting her personal problems and the misdeeds on the ranch. She wept for the ranch, for herself but primarily for her lost friend. April wept until her tears dried up leaving nothing but anger.

Struggling to her knees, she screamed at the squawking crows and berated the heavens as she carried the mangled farm dog home. With each step, the burden of the slight body weighed heavier on her arms, on her heart, until April succumbed to tears again. At last, she stumbled into the yard and collapsed at the end of the boardwalk, gently laying her friend on the grass. There, beside her lost friend, she wept until sleep overcame her.

APRIL WOKE up on the couch inside the house. She struggled to sit up.

"Relax," Wade suggested. "Don't be in a hurry to move. You carried Biscuit a long way. I sent the boys to follow the path you took. They didn't find anything, except the blood pool. You should have come back without her," he chided gently. "Or called in. You took your phone, right?"

She ignored the last question. It was stupid to go off without her phone, not to mention it being against ranch protocol to fail to carry some form of communication. Phone, walky-talky, radio. You never left the main yard without a way to be reached, or to call for help. "How could I leave her there for the crows and coyotes? She wasn't heavy, she's a small dog." April defended her actions, angry that Wade questioned her, angrier still that he was still here. "Why are you still here? I told you to leave."

"April, honey, Biscuit was small and light, but you're pregnant and only days ago took a strenuous ride and endangered that baby. You need to take care."

"How can I take care of my baby when my world is falling apart?" She didn't mean it; this baby was everything to her. The precious life she carried was more important than the ranch; but she was done in. Wasted from the continual stress. She lashed out because she didn't know what else to do.

"Let it go for now. We can deal with it later," he advised. "Everyone is waiting outside. We're going to bury Biscuit. Jack showed us where."

Numbly, she stumbled to her feet and let him lead her out of the house. He helped her onto a quad and drove her down the hill to a small field past the barn, where the guests and Jack were gathered beside a freshly dug hole.

She slid off the quad, nearly losing her balance. A strong hand at her elbow steadied her as Wade urged her forward. On the ground beside the hole was a small wooden box.

"A coffin?" She whispered brokenly.

"Jack said she was your favorite. I thought it fitting." Wade whispered.

Jack and Tommy lowered the box into the hole and everyone gently shoveled dirt overtop. Courtney placed a small cross with Biscuit's name on it above the hole while the other girls planted dandelions on top of the overturned dirt. Dandelions, spots of sunshine that turned to wishing flowers, an appropriate tribute to a fallen friend. She wept again for their kindness.

Wade cleared his throat. "I just want to take a moment to say thank you to Biscuit. I barely knew her, but she was always happy and greeted me eagerly. I've heard she was one of the best cow dogs around. She was a good friend and we're all sad to see her go. Run free, Biscuit. Enjoy puppy heaven, where food and water are plentiful and there are countless cows for chasing. Say hi to Grampa Morgan for us. You will be missed."

Everyone else said a quiet good-bye and they strolled sadly

toward the house. April stood for several long minutes, staring at the raw earth and flowers. Finally, she looked at Wade.

"Who made the coffin?" It should have been a simple question, but it felt like so much more. It carried the questions she couldn't ask, the ones she didn't dare express. But Wade took the question at face value.

"I did, while you slept. I knew you loved her. I didn't want you to see her looking like that again. I'm not much of a wood worker, but I did the best I could."

"Thank you," she whispered, climbing onto the quad. "Take me home, please."

"Your wish is my command."

They rode the short distance in silence, eventually joining everyone else in the kitchen. Supper was a subdued affair. They finished the meal with oatmeal raisin cookies, baked by Wade while April was gone walking.

"You made these?" April asked him.

"I did. It wasn't hard. I've baked before, though I don't like it much. My foster-mother helped me learn. And the supplies and recipe were out. I hoped I might earn brownie points," he added sheepishly.

She slanted a glance at him. "One brownie point earned. And four for the coffin. But I still think you should go."

"At the risk of earning your ire, again, I would like to stay out the two weeks I paid for, before I return to the hectic life I left."

The hint of pleading and caution in his voice reassured her that he knew he'd erred and was trying to make it right. "I don't know," she hesitated. She wanted him gone, yet she wanted him here. Damn her stupid heart.

"I am so sorry I didn't tell you who I was, who I am. I was enjoying being anonymous. Sometimes being semi-famous and having money has its drawbacks. You seemed to like me, not my name or my money. That was important to me. I chose not to jeopardize that. Although I realize it was a pretty damned stupid mistake for a man who prizes honesty more than almost anything else." He shrugged as if questioning his own stupidity.

She didn't answer him right away. She couldn't. He made her question her decision-making abilities. Having him here was nice, but the resultant tension was overwhelming. She was exhausted and devastated by yet another death. Finally, she chose not to decide. "I need to think about it. I'll let you know tomorrow, but don't get your hopes up. Good night, Wade."

"Do you want me to move to the bunkhouse with the others?"

She paused on the threshold of the stairs. "There's no sense making more work for later; the sheets need changed already. You might as well stay in the guest room. Lock the doors when you turn in, please."

WADE WATCHED her trudge up the stairs, her steps slow and weary. She looked every inch the heartbroken heroine from an old movie. He'd taken the spark and joy from her with his lies. Through all the trouble and losses she'd experienced this last week, she'd carried on with a smile. Sometimes it was a grin-and-bear-it-until-it-goes-away smile but her innate optimism had always shone through. But now, now that cheerfulness was extinguished like a candle in a hurricane. And he was to blame.

He was a colossal asshat.

He had to figure out a way to get past the damage he'd done and regain her trust. He'd start by letting the police know about Biscuit and by getting Rex to dig harder for information. It crossed his mind, again, that he might want more than just friendship with April. He could easily picture them in a relationship. But that could never work out. She was all country and he was a city-boy. He pushed any idea of permanence aside.

Rex's voice echoed in his head. There were options. Could he step down from the helm of WKB? Maybe he could work more with The Grace Foundation, the non-profit organization he'd formed in his birth mother's name. He used the inheritance, held in a trust fund, from his parents' death to start his own company. Now, with a portion of the profits from that, he provided funding, loans or grants to worthy small businesses to help them get on their feet. Was there a larger place for him in the charity? Could The Grace Foundation give him the purpose he'd lost to the hectic day-to-day drama of corporate life?

And could he run it from Wildwood? From the Lazy-W?

Technology had come a long way in the twelve years since he'd formed WKB. Working online was easy. E-mail, laptops and cell phones had changed the business landscape entirely. He could work from a home office, or even set up an office in town.

He chuckled wryly at his own arrogance and unreality. April was barely speaking to him, and they'd only met a week ago; and here he was thinking long term and considering changing his whole life for her. For them. Yeah, he was an idiot. Talk about jumping the gun.

It must be related to the protective feelings she roused in him. The image of her truck broken down on the side of the highway, her squatting beside it in the pouring rain, trying to hide what she was doing, brought a smile. She was tough, adorable and could laugh at herself. She was an intriguing puzzle he wanted to solve. How was he going to do that if she kicked him off the ranch?

He'd find a way to convince April to let him stay for the full two weeks because there was no way he'd leave a pregnant woman alone with only an old man for protection. The next gunshot that rang out could be aimed at her. He'd sleep in his truck on the road out to protect her. And he'd do his damndest to figure out who was behind all the bullshit going on.

CHAPTER TWENTY-TWO

"I'd like to stay on, if I could," Tommy stated at breakfast two days later. "I'll pay for another two weeks. My summer job fell through, so I'm in no rush to get back to the city."

"Are you crazy?" Ryan asked.

"Nope. I love it here. The peace and quiet, the animals, it feels like home. I might even look into changing my major to veterinary medicine."

"Man, you got shot! Animals have been killed. This place is a freaking war zone." Ryan's voice was heavy with disdain. "I can't wait to get out of here."

"I'd love to stay. I wish I could." Courtney piped up, and the others echoed her sentiment.

"I'm glad you enjoyed your visit, especially since it's been so crazy. I hope you'll pass along a good word or two," April requested.

"And leave out the shooting?" Courtney asked with a laugh.

"Hell yes," April agreed. "Best not to mention that."

"I'll keep it to myself, and I'll post a positive review on the new website, too. I'd like to come back during winter break as well. I'll e-mail you the dates so you can book me in. I can't wait to see this place covered in snow." She sighed blissfully.

"I'll do that, but at this point, I'm still not sure if we'll be up and running. You know the story. Things are still up in the air. If we ever figure out who is behind all this, I'd love to have you back. Tommy, you're welcome to stay on for a while longer."

"Awesome! I'll just drive these guys back to the city and pick up a few things and be back first thing in the morning. Can I bring you back anything?"

"I don't think so, but thanks."

April, Jack and Wade accompanied the group to their cars and watched them drive away.

Uncomfortable silence filled the air between April and Wade. She'd agreed, reluctantly to let him stay. She wasn't sure she liked the decision, but he was paying and she needed the money. She always needed the damned money, she just wished it wasn't coming from Wade.

"It feels like I'm saying good-bye to old friends," April said, melancholy filling her voice. "I really did enjoy them. I'm going to love running the Bale and if it works out, the Bed and Breakfast too."

"You can do it," Wade smiled at her.

His grin turned her insides liquid. Did the man have to be so devastatingly handsome and annoying at the same time?

"I don't want your money. But I do appreciate you letting Rex work for me."

"I don't understand how you can accept a pro-bono lawyer but won't accept a grant to provide operating capital."

"We've been over it a hundred times in the past two days. I won't take your money."

"Even if it isn't my money?"

"Let it go," she warned him. "I'm going for a ride." She held up a hand to forestall his objections. "A long, slow walk on a horse, no trotting or galloping. I won't even canter."

"I'll join you."

She glared. Didn't he realize she was trying to get away from him? It was impossible to think when he was around. He flustered her and knocked her logic off kilter. "No thank you," she responded after discarding several impolite responses.

"I'm not letting you go alone. The shooter could still be out there. Who knows what he's planning next? I'd feel better if I went with you."

"I would too," Jack added. The old hand's words sealed her fate. "And take a damned gun." He shook his finger at Wade. "And you remember what I told you about shootin'. Keep the safety on. Don't aim at anything you don't intend to kill. Keep your finger out of the trigger guard. And for God's sake, don't do anything stupid."

"Fine." She glared at Jack and ignored Wade, who'd been taking shooting lessons from Jack in the few spare moments they'd had between crises. She'd never admit it, but Wade had become a decent shot in a short time and had a healthy respect for firearms and safety.

She rode slowly along fence lines, through heavily treed areas, passing through several gates, leaving Wade to close them after he passed through. She didn't have a destination; she just wanted to ride and think. Thankfully, Wade kept his mouth shut and followed at a distance; close enough to keep watch but with enough distance he didn't impinge on her solitude. She was almost able to ignore him.

Without planning it, she ended up at the spring someone had enlarged to a bathing pool. The water wasn't hot, but it was warm and perfect for soaking in. Rock lined, with a comfortable seating edge and steps into the water, the pool was about ten feet in diameter and varied from knee deep to chest high. The pool stayed full, presumably from a small underground spring. It overflowed into a second basin disappearing from there. She wasn't certain why the dual pools seemed to fill from nowhere and didn't appear to drain yet were always fresh. She chalked it up to one of Mother Nature's wonders. She dismounted carefully and set her horse to graze.

Lush greenery, primarily pine and spruce trees, shaded the sun-dappled pool. Moss and ferns surrounded the rock edges. A picnic table and a high-backed wooden bench sat under the trees. Pine and sulphur filled the air. She slipped out of her shoes and socks, rolled up her jeans and picked her way slowly down the sandstone path to the edge and sat, dangling her feet in the water. She grunted at the tightness around her abdomen. Her belly hadn't grown much, but her old jeans were rapidly getting tighter. Soon, she'd have to up-size her clothing.

Wade dismounted, but he didn't join her.

"Come on," she invited reluctantly. "You might as well enjoy the water."

"Thank you." He chose a section of ledge nearby, but not too close, and sat with his feet hanging in the water.

It was nice that he respected her need for silence and kept his distance. She felt bad for being curt. But so many things kept knocking her askew. She felt like she was in a losing battle with an MMA fighter and had taken one too many punches.

"The moss over there is trampled flat," he pointed to the far side of the pool. "Do a lot of animals drink here?"

She looked up, startled, and studied the opposite side of the pool. "I've never seen a one. I think the sulphur keeps them away. I've only ever seen tracks during a drought."

"Do you think we should check it out?"

The words were more a statement than a question. They felt like an olive branch. She nodded and they slipped into their shoes.

"Those are boot prints," she exclaimed. "Someone's worn a path to the pond." She started following it. Wade grabbed his rifle and jogged to catch up. She didn't want to know what or rather who they'd find. For a moment, she wished Wade would take the lead. They hadn't kept their voices quiet, so anyone in the vicinity would have heard them and fled.

They followed the well-travelled, twisting path for about five hundred yards to an old line-shack April had forgotten even existed. Crafted from heavy logs, an eternity ago, it stood strong and humble in a grove of pines. She pushed the door open and peeked inside. Clumps of mud littered the floor. A jumble of clothes teetered on a chair, throw away dishes were stacked everywhere and a ratty old sleeping bag lay on the bed.

"Someone's living here," Wade exclaimed.

April jerked back and banged her head into his chin. "Ouch. Don't sneak up on me," she growled, rubbing away the sting.

The interior log walls were worn smooth with age, the

chinking was cracked in places but overall, the cabin was sound and weatherproof. Sunlight filtered through a grubby, four-paned window, illuminating the filthy interior. Upended cardboard boxes and old crates served as table and cupboards. A battered military trunk, half covered by clutter, peeked out from behind a straight-backed chair. April hurried over and knelt in front the familiar trunk. It used to be in the house. It was Grampa Morgan's Army trunk. He'd done a brief stint in the Army as a young man.

"It's locked."

"Let me see." Wade hunkered down beside her. "I don't suppose you have a hair pin?"

"Wait. The key," she exclaimed and pulled the old key she'd found under her grandfather's bed from around her neck. "Try this."

Wade pushed it into the lock and attempted to turn it. "It fits, but it doesn't work. The mechanism must be scarred." He handed the key back to her without looking as he examined the locking mechanism. "How about that hairpin?"

She extracted a bobby pin from her braid and passed it over. He straightened it, bent the tip and jammed it into the lock. After a few minutes of twisting and jiggling, he popped the lock open.

"Oh, my God, why do you know how to do that?"

"Saw it on *MacGyver* reruns. You should see me with a rubber band, a paper clip and a lighter," he quipped and flipped the fastener open and lifted the lid. Pristine packages of white powder lay in immaculate rows at one end of the trunk. The other two-thirds was filled with handguns and ammunition.

April gasped in shock.

"Drugs? Who the hell is stockpiling drugs on my ranch?" Grabbing the corner of a white paper sticking out from under the guns, she pulled out a hand-written note about an upcoming meeting. It didn't say about what or with who, but the date, time and location were right there in black and white. And only days from now.

"I know this handwriting. This is Uncle John's."

"Guess he's not dead," Wade quipped.

"I guess not. What the hell is he up to? And why is he selling drugs? What if he's the wily bastard who's been shooting at us?" The blood rushed from her head and she teetered on her knees, listing badly to the left before regaining her equilibrium. What if she'd come alone and her uncle had found her?

"We better get out of here before he comes back. Who knows where he is now?" Wade slipped a package of drugs into his jacket pocket. "Proof for the police," he advised when she raised her eyebrows at him.

They mounted and headed straight back to the home quarter. Birds twittered and chirped in the trees and an eagle soared down the length of the path, searching for food. A light breeze wafted through the branches, setting the leaves whispering. April's mind flittered between the beauty around her and the crazy thoughts running amok in her mind. Eventually, her attention turned fully inside her head wondering why...

Why had her uncle disappeared? Why was he selling drugs? Why did everyone seem to think he was dead and not just missing? It was crazy; it didn't make any sense. She rode along slowly, comfortable with the sedate, safe, pace as an idea formed in her mind. What was the missing piece, the link that tied everything together? She kept her musings to herself for the time being.

BEHIND APRIL, Wade kept watch on their surroundings. They couldn't risk riding unaware. Despite his vigilance, he found he watched her more than their surroundings. She drew his gaze like a moth to a flame. He couldn't keep away. Pregnant, strong, beautiful, intelligent. April Cooper had it all. Finding those drugs must have shaken her to the core, but she showed few signs of distress, beyond her unusual silence and the rigid set of her shoulders. That outward calm was a lie. In only a week, he'd recognized she internalized and processed things before revealing them to the world. Sure, sometimes she just blurted her thoughts out, but that wasn't her usual fashion, unless she was nervous.

She kept her head in a crisis, and that was admirable.

They'd have to call the police. Again. Sergeant Miller would be ambivalent at best. There was something up with him too. This whole place was tied into one tight, writhing ball of snakes. At least the guests had departed. That meant eight less backs to guard. Protecting April would be easier now…if he could focus, because watching her was a pleasure and a distraction. He studied her as she rode ahead of him. She swayed gently with the motion of the horse. Her braided hair swung back and forth across her shoulders, tempting him to touch it, to wrap it around his hand and draw her close.

Whoa!

Don't go there!

He wasn't interested in testing the physical water with

April. No way, no how. He should have left long before now. But watching her ride, her slim body and tight little backside stirred longings he hadn't felt in months, maybe years. The attraction was undeniable, and not purely physical, though he was loath to admit it. She touched something inside him, something that hadn't been affected in a long time.

They needed to solve the mystery of the Lazy-W so he could get the hell out of here before he became irrevocably tangled in her life at the expense of his own.

Yeah, because his life was so stellar right now. Too many political dinners where he tried in vain to convince politicians the oil and gas business wasn't evil. Oil companies were becoming increasingly environmentally conscious and had started improving how they cleaned up their sites and the way they did business. The industry wasn't perfect, but it was improving as quickly as new technology allowed. Unfortunately, many people refused to admit the truth of that.

And Lord help him, since his breakup, too many dinner dates with scheming women intent on trapping him into marriage and getting their hands on his money. Wasn't there a woman out there, anywhere, who wanted Wade Kelly Borne the man, not the billionaire?

April turned back to look at him. "Come on, Borne, get that city slicker butt in gear. You're falling behind."

Okay, maybe there was one woman who saw the man, not the money. His lips curved upward. Yeah, April was different from the rest. Good different.

～

Sergeant Miller arrived with six officers to search the cabin and outbuildings for further signs of drugs. With the other officers investigating, April sat at the kitchen table while Miller, his back resting against the wall, took her statement.

Wade handed over the note and drugs he'd removed from the trunk and leaned negligently against the counter, a steaming coffee mug cradled in his hands. He looked delicious standing there. Strong. Masculine. Confident. He looked like…someone she could lean on.

"I don't like this," Miller snapped at April, jerking her attention back to the conversation. "How do I know this isn't your doing? How do I know you aren't the person responsible for the rise in drug use in Wildwood?" He glared at her, his brows pinched together, his lips downturned and clamped together. As head of the Edson RCMP detachment, Wildwood and the surrounding area fell under his command.

"Are you insane?" April blurted. "If I was trafficking drugs, would I call you? Would I have asked for an investigation? I just want the drugs off my land. I want people to stop shooting the ones I love. I want a normal life."

"Missy, that's an awful lot to ask for. Especially with all the shenanigans going on here," Miller growled.

Wade stepped forward, putting himself between April and Miller, like he had the day he arrived. Was it only nine days ago? It felt like he'd been here much longer than that.

"Listen to me, Miller. April has done nothing wrong here. In fact, I'm beginning to question your ability to act as an impartial investigator in this matter. Get your shit together or I'll put in a call to your superiors and have another officer sent out."

April's mouth dropped open. She snapped it closed. Wade

was calm and rational, but there was no doubt he'd do exactly as he'd threatened. He was a man used to getting his way and had enough sway in the province to get what he wanted. Funny, he'd always seemed competent, but she was recognizing the reason his business was so successful. He had power, personal and business power. Never mind his charisma and raw sexuality. Right now, he was a complete and total alpha-male, and man-oh-man, he was steaming her hormones.

She shook her head and rose from her chair. "Sergeant Miller, please just investigate this. Do what you need to do. Find out who's living in that cabin, it might be my uncle, and get rid of those drugs, before I burn them myself." His attitude was annoying and perplexing and frankly, she'd had enough of it.

"Your uncle is missing, presumed dead," Miller countered.

"April says the note is in John Wyatt's handwriting. That could mean he's alive and hiding here on the ranch. It might also explain the stolen cattle we found, the dead bull, the dead dog, the shots at people…" He paused. "With the date and times on that note, you've got two days to set a trap and potentially capture the culprit." Wade gave Miller a hard look. "I get that you're angry over something. I have no idea what it is, but don't let that hinder your investigation here."

"Wade," April said warningly. What was he doing? Was he trying to anger Miller? He needed to back down now, before Miller got annoyed and left. While he was unlikely to abandon the investigation, if he was pissed off, Miller might not give it his best effort.

Wade's gaze pivoted from Miller to April. She raised one eyebrow at him.

Slowly, he stepped back and resumed his casual stance against the counter. "I apologize, Sergeant Miller. I'm worried for the safety of everyone here and when the drugs disappear, things could escalate."

"Point taken," Miller conceded grudgingly with a nod. "I'm short on officers right now, but this is important. I'll juggle some schedules and try to get some overtime approved for extra manpower. Maybe I can borrow from another detachment. You're an important man in the province. I might be able to make a case for you being a dignitary." He glanced at Wade.

"He's leaving." April stated, hoping Wade would agree and not argue with her.

"I'll stay," Wade countered. "What kind of man would leave you alone in a situation like this? So, unless you want to leave with me, you're stuck with me for a while longer." He offered his hand to Miller. "Thanks, I appreciate this."

Provided with maps of every building and hidey hole on the ranch, they'd searched for hours. The only sign of habitation was in the old cabin. Miller had an officer hidden in a portable tree stand with a clear view of the cabin. In a change of plans, the guns, the drugs, a cell phone, truck keys and rifle found hidden under the bed were left there to avoid tipping off the cabin's resident.

It was well after dark, nearing midnight, when the RCMP officers were finally gone. April watched them go, too keyed up to sleep. She settled onto the oversized leather couch in the living room and turned on the television.

"The fireplace channel?" Wade asked.

"DVD. No cable out here. There used to be satellite..." She didn't complete the sentence. He'd already heard the poor-me litany a thousand times and she was getting sick of repeating it. "I love a fire, but it's too hot for a real one… crazy, though, I'm cold. Like I have a chill I can't shake."

Probably fear and uncertainty, she decided. Her life had been tough and up in the air since she'd been accused of the drug thefts. Things just seemed to keep going downhill. Like she was on a slippery slope and couldn't stop. Or like she was in quicksand and was slowly, inexorably going under. Wade was the only bright spot on the horizon, but his presence here was temporary as well. A soft, tired sigh escaped her and she dropped her head back and closed her eyes.

CHAPTER TWENTY-THREE

ade made hot chocolate with whipped cream and marshmallows for them both. He really wanted a stiff drink, but that wasn't happening. He wanted his faculties intact for whatever happened next. Plus, he rarely drank alone, no matter how badly he felt the need. He'd lost a few good executives to alcohol, some after he paid for their rehab. Instead, he put the mugs on a towel-covered cookie sheet, added a couple napkins, a plate of cookies and some expensive chocolates from the stash he'd picked up in town and carried the tray into the living room.

April slumped in the corner of the couch, a light blanket over her legs. She fidgeted with a leather coaster, spinning it between her fingers.

"Here, I brought you a snack. That baby needs you to keep up your strength, and you hardly ate supper." He waited for her to shift positions. When she sat upright with her feet braced on the coffee table, he eased onto the opposite end of the battered black leather couch and set the tray between them.

"Thanks. It was hard to eat with the cops coming and going all the time. Besides, I don't really have an appetite. The tension is killing my stomach. I swear that sometimes my guts are going to come spewing out."

Wade laughed sympathetically. "Now, there's an image." He paused. "Honestly, how has your nausea been? I haven't seen you being sick for a couple days. Are you done? Or just hiding it?"

"Thankfully, I seem to be finished, for now, at least. I'm sick of being sick, and today taxed my stomach's control." She picked up her mug and picked a mini-marshmallow off the top and popped it into her mouth. "Marshmallows and whipped cream?"

"What can I say, I have a major sweet tooth and you need the calories. I could make you a sandwich or something else…" He'd do whatever was necessary to get her to eat.

She shook her head, scooped up a dollop of topping and popped it into her mouth.

Wade stared, mesmerized. Didn't she know what she was doing? Dear God. Nothing like a beautiful, sexy woman sucking something to distract a man and send his blood flow straight to his groin. He crossed his legs to hide the effect she was having on him. She swirled her tongue around her finger, scooping up another bit of whipped cream. He forced himself to turn away and watch the mock fire. He would not stare at her. He refused to torture himself like that, or to denigrate her and make her into a sex object. That wasn't who he was, despite rumors in the paper about his *dating* history. Barely able to keep his gaze averted, Wade took a moment to check the e-mails on his phone.

"So," he began awkwardly. "Remember when Werner said

he was working for Triad Resorts? I called an old university chum who works for Triad. Triad wants the land because someone told them about the mineral spring. They plan to build a resort here. Nobody seems to know who told them about the spring. I had Rex hire an investigator. All we could determine was that it was an anonymous tip. He's still investigating. Something isn't on the up-and-up here."

"Why is everyone set on getting me off this land? Shootings, rustlers, drugs? My entire world is falling apart." She huffed out a breath.

"The question is, who has the most to gain if you sell? Besides, Triad," Wade offered. "Who knew about the spring?"

"Besides everyone in the area? My uncle and my ex are the ones who come to mind first." Her eyes went wide and she clutched her hand to her chest. "Geez," she cried. "My ex has a drug problem. He framed me for drug thefts at the hospital. He knew Uncle John. What if they were working together? You know—drugs for information? If the land was sold, and Uncle John came back from the dead, he'd get everything…if he produced the will. He's the last known heir. Except that I'd get a cut, my father's share."

"Didn't your uncle already have everything? Why would he fake his death to get the land?" Wade puzzled aloud.

"But if those are his drugs and he's caught up in the drug trade, it might be his escape plan."

"We need to tell Miller about that first thing in the morning. And if you don't object, I'd like to have my investigator do some more digging."

"Now you ask?" She raised one eyebrow and guilt flooded through him.

He winced. "I apologize for that. I just wanted to help."

April turned to glare at him. She stood and paced circles around the coffee table, forcing him to draw in his legs with every lap. The investigation itself wasn't the issue. She resented Wade acting without asking her.

"I just wanted to help," she mimicked. "More likely you didn't want your famous-self tied up with a loser like me."

"It wasn't like that." It really hadn't been. He'd been trying to help.

She silenced him with a glare. "And what else did you have investigated? Me? Did you find out all my dirty little secrets? That I've been accused of stealing drugs? That my career is ruined and I'll never work as a nurse again? I tried to fight the dismissal, but my nurse's union won't help and Legal Aide has refused me because I might own the ranch. The fact I can't sell the ranch because I don't own it doesn't matter to them. Net worth and bottom line are all they care about. I suppose that's all that matters to you too. Image and money?"

She flopped on the couch and buried her face in her hands.

"Why didn't you ask me what you wanted to know?" she asked between her fingers. "Or is the great and powerful Borne too important to ask mere mortals for the facts? Does it make you feel superior to just do whatever you want with no regard for privacy?"

"It wasn't like that," he blustered.

"Save the lies. You told me you hated liars. How very hypocritical of you. Sneaking around behind my back, running investigations. How do I know you aren't after my land too? You did know the value of land in the area." She held up a hand, forestalling his objections. "Don't say a word. As soon as Miller traps whoever is doing this, you're gone.

Out of my life, out of my world. Take your money, your lawyer, and your investigator and get the hell off my land."

She stomped toward the hallway. Whirling around in the doorway, she pinned him with a sad look. "And how the hell did your ex-girlfriend know you were here?"

That was a very good question. How had Barbie known where to find him? He'd bet his last dollar April's ex had something to do with that. What was her ex up to now? And what was Barbara up to? Did she have some connection to April's ex? She must be tied into this somehow. She'd always had one eye on Paul Paulson, primary owner and CEO of Triad Resorts. But how had Triad learned about the issues here and why was Barbara hanging around Triad's errand boy?

CHAPTER TWENTY-FOUR

The next morning, Wade stood in the ranch kitchen and stared at his phone. "Rex, can you repeat that? You did what?"

"I hired a ranch hand and put him on your payroll." Rex's chuckle came through the phone loud and clear.

"And who approved this?"

"You did, when you gave me your proxy. I found him through Waterson Ripley Reece. He's an experienced ranch hand and a former US Marine. His wife was Canadian and he's looking to move into the Wildwood area. Wants their kids to know her family. I had Jack interview him over the phone. Jack's okay with him. Name's Billy Lewis. He'll be doing double duty as ranch hand and guard. Something smells rotten here and until April's good for nothing uncle is found, I intend to protect her."

"If you're protecting her, why is he on my payroll?"

"Because you're as rich as Midas, and I'm just a poor ol' lawyer." Rex laughed.

Wade rolled his eyes. "And where is this paragon now?"

"Told me he was getting his kids set up at their grandparents'. He'll be at the ranch today. Perhaps you can give him a cabin to live in. Just him for now, kids are staying with his folks until this settles out."

"Why didn't I know this before now?" He couldn't decide if he was pleased or irked by Rex's initiative. Plus, when this guy showed up, he'd have to explain it to April, putting him further into hot water. He raked his hand through his hair and twisted his neck to relieve the tension lodged at the base of his skull.

"Look, you assigned me to fix this. This is the start of a solution."

"Anything else I need to know?"

"Ya," Jack's voice came through the screen door. "We're outta milk. I made a grocery list and you're on grocery duty. Plus, I've got a hankering for some Chinese food. And you might want to wash your truck," Jack deadpanned. "I brought the plug-in cooler in to keep the perishables cold for the trip and if you wrap the Chinese in a blanket, it'll stay warm." He ambled away.

When Wade returned his attention to the phone, Rex was laughing.

"You trust this Marine?" Wade asked.

"His CO says he's the best. And I've confirmed his reputation through some connections. I think he's our best shot. Killing two birds with one stone. Well, I'm due in court, so I have to go. Keep me posted. Bye."

Wade once again stared at his phone. Nine in the morning and this day had not gone how he expected.

Someone knocked and a tall, lean man with a hard look and limp strolled into the kitchen. "Jack said to come introduce myself. I'm William Lewis. Call me Billy. Mr. Tremble hired me." He offered Wade his hand. "Nice to meet you, Mr. Borne." He grinned. "I guess, technically, you hired me."

They shook hands.

"I've been filled in on the situation. I'm leaving my kids at the in-laws until this mess is sorted out. I won't have them under fire if I can help it."

Wade studied the ex-Marine. Early thirties, clean cut, muscular and fit, he looked ready for action. His military experience would be an asset under these difficult conditions. And if he knew ranching, he was a definite bonus. Rex vetted him, and that was good enough for Wade.

"Consider yourself hired for the duration. After that, all ranch decisions are up to Miss Cooper. Nice to meet you, Billy. I'll leave you to ask Jack what needs done. Stick close to the main yard and keep your eyes open."

"Morning," April smiled as she entered the kitchen. "I can't believe I slept so late." She looked around. The room was empty except for a stranger. A tall, wiry stranger with half a dozen tattoos. Her smile morphed into a frown and her brows scrunched together uncomfortably. "Oh. Hi. I'm April and you are?" She let the question dangle. Fear skittered down her spine. Who the hell was this guy and why was he in her house? She inched toward the butcher's block on the counter. This guy was enormous, and tough looking. A knife might be her only way to beat him in a fight.

"Billy Lewis. Nice to meet you, ma'am. Mr. Tremble sent me to help out."

She growled lowly. Now what? When would people stop thinking she couldn't handle her life and when would they stop thrusting solutions at her and spending money she didn't have? Where the hell was Wade?

"Well, Billy. You might as well pack up and go. I can't afford to pay you."

"No worries, ma'am." He removed his battered Stetson and slapped it on his thigh. "Said to tell you this is a loan. He'll expect repayment when things settle down. And it ain't no good sending me away. I'm a former US Marine. Served my country for eight years. Got a few battle scars to show for it. Some crazy relative isn't scaring me away. I'm here to protect and serve."

She yanked her cell phone out of her jeans pocket and dialed Rex who confirmed he'd hired the cowboy. She gave Rex hell. They argued back and forth until she caved.

"I'd also like to do some ranching. It's been a long time since the kids and I rode a horse." He chuckled.

"Kids?" She squeaked. "You brought kids here. Dear God. Will this nightmare never end? Coffee! I need coffee." She didn't know whether to appreciate or resent Rex's interference. She definitely regretted letting Wade bring her home. Okay, maybe not. He'd been helpful in a lot of ways. But with his money and take-charge attitude, she was feeling pushed aside.

"Okay," she said, after swilling half a cup of coffee. "Did you, or did you not bring children to this ranch?"

"Well, yes and no," the tall, lean cowboy said. "I was looking for a way to emigrate to Canada. My dead wife's folks live nearby. Mine are passed. Wanted the kids to know their family. I had feelers out everywhere. Mr. Tremble hired me and is getting me the permits I need. The kids are at my in-laws. If this job works out, I'll be considering bringing them here to live, if that suits. If not, I'll be investigating other options."

"Well, that's a blessing. I wouldn't want to put your children in harm's way. I don't suppose there's any point in asking you to leave?"

"No, ma'am. Been paid an advance to come here. You're stuck with me until Mr. Tremble lets me go."

"Fine," she agreed reluctantly. There was no escaping the dominating men that had exploded into her life. Strangely though, as overprotective as this felt, it also felt right. Helping a man find his family. Giving him a job and getting someone with fighting experience to help keep everyone safe until her disaster of a life was straightened out. Yeah, her mind knew it was right, even if her pride bucked against it. "Put your things in the bunkhouse. You'll stay there...for the time being. We'll discuss your possible future here later. When and if this works out."

WADE HAD RETURNED from his grocery run into town, without the takeout Jack had requested. Tommy, delayed by family issues, had finally made it back. He was in the workshop with Wade, keeping busy doing who-knew-what while April stayed indoors, pacing and fretting. She couldn't find the focus for accounting, and sorting ancient paperwork had gotten old real fast. Billy stood guard on the front porch. Today was the date on the note from the trunk.

Everyone was poised for action but stuck in a holding pattern.

April pushed through the screen door onto the front porch. "Do you want coffee?" she asked her ad hoc ranch hand.

"That would be lovely, ma'am. Strong and black, please." He didn't take his eyes off his surroundings. "Can you bring it here? And one for the police officer out back too? We can't leave our posts until we hear from Miller."

"How did your wife die?" she asked when she returned with his coffee a few moments later. "If you don't mind sharing."

"Cancer. She had recurring bouts of skin cancer since she was a kid. It was in remission for almost six years. After Maisy was born, she's the youngest, it hit hard. Breast cancer she didn't even know she had metastasized into her lungs. Took her from us in two years. So now it's just the three of us. Cody is four and Maisy is three."

She placed a hand on his arm. "That's sad, but I'm glad you have the chance to let them meet their grandparents. And I'm grateful you can be here for me." Simple words; inadequate to express the emotions involved.

Such a tragedy. A family torn apart by cancer. April said a silent thank you that it had never touched anyone she loved. She'd known loss, too much of it. At times, her life hadn't been easy. But overall, she was blessed.

"Get inside," Billy demanded.

Something in his tone warned her not to argue. She skittered inside the house and closed the door behind her. Following pre-arranged protocol, she hurried upstairs and hid in the closet. She hated hiding but had reluctantly agreed to hide to protect her unborn child.

"This is ridiculous," she whispered, pulling the closet door shut behind her. Even as she grumbled, she hunkered down on the pile of pillows in the corner and pulled some clothing over to hide behind. She was frustrated, irritated and scared spitless, but she'd much rather be outside defending herself and her property than hiding in a closet like some namby-pamby wimp.

The silence was deafening. No voices, no footsteps. It was unnaturally quiet. Any other day, the lack of sound would have been bliss. Today it grated on her nerves. Her fists bunched, her toes tapped and her shoulders tensed. This wasn't good.

"Relax, Cooper," she whispered. Good gravy, she had to relax before this tension ripped her in two. She felt like she was being mentally drawn and quartered. Pulled in every direction at once. Tremors of fear and tension scraped up and down her spine. She twisted on her pile of pillows, unable to sit still.

As a nurse, she'd learned the best way to relax was meditation. She shifted positions to lean back against the wall, her legs crossed in front of her. Closing her eyes, she started deep breathing and visualizing a grass-filled meadow. Blue skies, birds chirping and flying high overhead, soaring high and swooping lazily back down. A warm breeze drifting over her skin. Her breathing slowed and became even. She wasn't calm, by any stretch, but she was mildly less tense and that was a start.

A gunshot shattered the silence and a small squeak escaped her. She burrowed deeper into the closet, all illusions of calm evaporating in an instant. A thousand crazy scenarios ricocheted through her mind, freezing her in place. Her fight or flight response kicked in big time. Run? Hide? Adrenaline flooded her system; her extremities tingled in its wake.

Her heart pounded.

Blood thundered through her veins.

Her breathing accelerated.

She was twitchy, almost unable to fight the urge to move. Only fear for her baby kept her in place.

Shouts echoed through the house. The front door slammed. Someone raced through the house and out the back door. It bounced twice before closing. April clenched her fists together to keep from bolting.

"Oh God. Oh God. Oh God," she whispered. "Dear God, let me get through this. Keep me safe. Keep us all safe." It wasn't a prayer, exactly, more a plea for help and calm. Rational thought was impossible. She rocked back and forth, willing herself to relax and remain alert.

"You'll never take me alive," a panicked masculine voice hollered somewhere outside. A barrage of high-powered rifle shots shattered the stillness after his words. Silence dropped deafeningly.

A door banged. Footsteps pounded up the stairs.

She burrowed back farther.

The closet door exploded open and a masculine hand reached inside. She screamed and started punching. She punched and kicked, scraping her nails across anything she could reach. She was yanked from the closet and a hand clamped over her mouth. She bit down hard, tasting the coppery tang of blood. Her captor cursed and pushed her away.

Ducking under his arms, she bolted for the stairwell.

"Dammit, April. Get back here!" Wade hollered at her.

She was halfway down the stairs when the words registered. She stumbled to a stop at the bottom, her heart thrashed about in her chest and her breath came in gasps. Bile rose in her throat. Dammit, she was going to be sick.

She swallowed hard and staggered into the kitchen. She felt like her body was on fire. Leaning against the counter, she ran cold water over her wrists and focused on deep breathing to still her heartbeat and calm her stomach.

With some semblance of rationality restored, she rinsed her mouth, repeatedly, with warm water and turned to face Wade. He'd come into the room just after her.

"You, princess, are a spitfire. I never would have guessed a little thing like you could fight like that. Another inch to the left and I'd never have kids. You damn near kicked my balls clean off." He chuckled.

She blushed. "Sorry."

"Don't be," he advised. "I should have announced myself. You must have been terrified."

"Are you okay?"

"Mostly. I think I'll need a bandage and some antibiotic cream for this bite." He held out his left hand, showing her a ring of teeth marks, several of which had punctured the skin at the base of his thumb.

"Oh-my-God," she cried out, reaching for his hand. "I'm so sorry."

"You're like a cornered badger," he laughed. "Remind me never to frighten you again."

"What happened?" she whispered, hating the way her voice trembled with the aftermath of fear.

"I'm not sure yet. I was on my way up from the barn when all hell broke loose. We need to stay inside until we get the all-clear. I just know someone got shot. Billy said it was safe for you to leave the closet. I was coming to get you."

They cleaned and bandaged Wade's hand and then sat side by side on the couch, wordlessly enduring the silence until someone could come with news. With the drapes closed, the darkness amplified the intimacy of being together, and the fear of what was happening outside. The waiting was interminable.

Half an hour passed.

Tommy and Billy came into the house.

"Holy crap," Tommy exclaimed. "You won't believe this!"

Billy sighed. "Miller killed his own son. Boy was out of control. High as a kite on something. Threatening to burn the house down. He fired the first shot." Billy shook his head. "Miller had no choice. He had to stop him before anyone else got hurt. I don't think he meant to kill him, just slow him down. Miller's in his squad car, waiting for a superior officer from the city. Someone else has to lead this investigation now. Sad that this had to happen. Damn drugs. Kid claimed the drugs were his. Said your uncle was dead. Not sure it's the truth, but he swore it was true with his last breath."

He went on to explain that someone had knocked out the man guarding the cabin, tied him up and taken the drugs. The officer was fine now, but somewhat chagrinned by being caught unaware.

"This has been the best damned vacation. Ever. But I hope the shooting's stopped." Tommy flopped into a chair.

• • •

HOURS LATER, April dropped, exhausted, onto the couch. She'd spent the day feeding cops, helping them where they needed it and answering a gazillion questions. If she had to answer another one, she'd rip her hair out. A cup of tea with a sandwich and brownie perched on the saucer appeared in front of her. She looked up.

Wade smiled at her. "You need sustenance. You didn't eat much today."

"A brownie?" She chuckled weakly.

"Tommy brought them and you do love chocolate. You should eat the sandwich first. Are you going to be okay?" He kneeled in front of her, his hands on her knees.

His touch was gentle, his hands warm. She felt like she'd never be warm again. Such insanity, such craziness. Her life had gone to hell in just weeks. Her uncle and her grandfather dead. The ranch in debt, the will missing. Nobody in control. Hopefully Rex Tremble would be able to get things going. She couldn't survive in limbo much longer. She was going to have to get a job. But doing what? Her reputation as a nurse was ruined. No hospital or clinic would hire her. Cashier? Waitress? Neither held much appeal, but she'd do what she had to.

"What are you thinking?" he asked quietly.

"Options. I think I'll have to get a job, at least until the baby comes."

"Or sell some cattle. That would bring in some income to get by on while Rex does his thing. Or accept the grant."

"It's just that easy for you, isn't it?" she demanded. "Money to burn and throw away at lost causes? Here, have a few bucks. It'll solve everything. I've already accepted the 'loan' of a hired gunman, oh sorry, a ranch hand." The constant tension was shaking her rationality. She wanted to lash out and hit something. She pushed him away, stood and slammed her tea onto the table. Her grandmother's antique cup rattled alarmingly on the saucer and the food dropped off onto the floor; she didn't care.

The man was a colossal ass if he thought he could just throw money around and make things right. Didn't he get it? Didn't he see her life was imploding? No job, her home and history in jeopardy. She was alone and lost. Hell, she could even face false charges for drug theft if her ex and his lover, her former boss, decided to play ugly. They'd played fast and loose with her reputation once before; nothing said they wouldn't try again if they had something they wanted from her.

"Tommy's here. He's paying to help for a month. That'll help with the income and the chores. Billy's here too."

"I suppose," she agreed sadly. "It's just so…so…crazy. I can't cope."

"Maybe you need to talk to someone after all this settles out."

Great, now he thought she needed a shrink. It just got better and better. She felt it coming, the slide into a well of self-pity. She had to break out of this mindset before it sucked her down into a well she couldn't get out of. Depression had a way of sneaking up on a person, and with pregnancy making her hormones run amuck, she could, potentially, be susceptible. He was right. She might need to talk this over with someone, but she'd try talking to Beth first. Sometimes friends could be as much help as a professional.

Under different circumstances, Wade might have been a good person to talk to. But her attraction to him had been forged under difficult circumstances, and that made for strange bed-fellows. Oh good, now she was thinking of him in terms of bed. She suppressed a sigh. If it weren't for his enormous wealth and the fact he lived four hours away, she might be interested in pursuing a relationship with him.

Ha. As if he'd be interested in a country mouse like her. Nope city-boy was going to disappear in the night and never look back. Besides, their ideals were miles apart. No sense pinning her wishes and dreams on that star.

WADE WATCHED HER EXPRESSIONS. "LOOK," Wade interrupted her musings. "I have to go back to Calgary for a day. Something's come up that I have to handle. I won't be gone more than a day. Two at most. You should be okay here. The drugs are gone, Miller's son is out of the picture and you've got Tommy, Jack and Billy to watch over things."

"Go ahead," Her voice rattled with resignation.

She wasn't happy he was leaving. Good. He wanted her to miss him. But, if it wasn't for needing to be present in person for the upcoming discussion, he'd rather stay here and keep her safe, within his sight. He'd miss her, even if he was only gone for hours. And, not just because he was worried about her safety. He'd miss April Cooper, the beautiful, strong, sexy rancher who could fight her way through anything. He just hoped she'd fight for him, not against him when she realized what he was up to.

CHAPTER TWENTY-FIVE

April stepped around Sage and Dalton, the two remaining cattle dogs, patting each one on the head as she moved on to another stall. She brushed Charlie Chaplin's coat to shining and released the horse to graze in the adjoining paddock. Grooming the horses was supposed to be a diversion for her overactive mind. Usually there was something soothing in the repetitive action of brushing each one down and checking their hooves and shoes. Today the mindless work left her heart free to drag her brain in unwanted directions.

The vision of Wade saying good-bye last week made her weepy. He said he'd be gone a day or two. Six days had passed and he hadn't come back. He'd called twice to check on things, but it felt—inadequate. It was illogical that seeing his truck lights fade in the distance should leave a gaping hole in her heart. The man was an enigma. So kind and helpful but also deceptive. What was he up to? Why hadn't he explained his need to return to the city? Why couldn't he just have admitted who he was in the first place?

Because then she'd have treated him differently and likely refused to allow him to remain on the Lazy-W. That would have been a shame. With the barrage of disasters raining down on her, he'd been a rock, grounding her, helping her weather the storm. He'd picked up the reins and taken control when she floundered. He'd rescued her countless times. He'd cooked and cleaned and learned to do chores. He'd been her protector.

Good grief, why had she let him go?

"Because there's no life for his city ways on the ranch," she mumbled. Heck, there might not even be a ranch if Rex couldn't get things moving. He reported in every few days, typically to inform her there was nothing to report. It was disheartening at best. Beth had visited numerous times, almost daily. April appreciated that. But as lovely and amusing as Beth was, she was no substitute for Wade.

Boots and Mittens, the two most domesticated barn cats stroked themselves around her ankles. She released the last horse into the paddock and she dropped to her bottom in the middle of the aisle and drew the persistent cats onto her lap. Tears running down her cheeks, she hugged them close, seeking comfort in their presence and soft fur.

Barking their heads off, the dogs raced from the barn in pursuit of something. Startled, the cats scrambled to safety. April paid them no heed. If she had company, she didn't care. Wade was gone and wasn't coming back. Eventually, the dogs quieted and soft footfalls could be heard coming down the center aisle. Probably Jack or Tommy.

She didn't turn to greet her guest. Frankly, she didn't care who it was.

"Bitch!" a voice growled.

Pain exploded through her head and everything went black.

~

Twitchy with anticipation, Wade put the pedal to the metal on his way back to the ranch. He was certain to get a ticket, or a fast driving award, as one of his staff called them. He had two windows down, the fresh country air washing the stench of the city from his lungs. The past week had been a whirlwind of activity. He should be exhausted, but excitement ruled the day. He had so much to share with April. He just hoped she'd listen.

Rounding the curve and passing under the gate, the acrid smell of smoke assaulted his nose. Something was on fire! He glanced up to see billowing plumes of smoke and ash and flames a hundred feet high.

"Shit!" It was the barn. He crossed the last distance as fast as he dared, slammed on the brakes, the rear end of his truck fishtailing, nearly passing the hood as he slid to a stop a short distance away. Throwing it into park, he leaped out and raced toward the towering inferno. Half the barn was consumed in flames and smoke billowed everywhere.

Jack and Billy came sprinting around the corner. "The horses are all out, but I can't find April," Jack called out.

Wade's heart stopped and exploded into double-time beating. "Where was she?" He paused in front of the old hand.

"Grooming the horses." Jack's face paled and he wobbled on his feet. "Maybe she's still inside." He clutched his chest and gasped for breath.

"Sit," Wade ordered and bolted headlong into the wide-open barn door.

The heat was oppressive, searing his face. The smoke stole the air from his lungs as he tried to call her name. Deep in the barn, barely discernible through the roar of the fire, came a sharp bark. Hardly able to see through watering eyes, Wade stumbled forward, his heart in his throat. Timbers creaked and groaned; windows exploded. The fire flared, growing hotter and hotter. His skin dried and ached.

The bark sounded again. He pulled his T-shirt up over his mouth and nose and stumbled blindly forward until he tripped over something soft. The dog nipped at him and he yanked his hand back. The dog, he couldn't see which one, snagged his jeans and tugged.

"Okay, boy," Wade coughed. "Show me."

With little nips at his ankles, the dog herded Wade forward, barking weakly until Wade bumped against something. Dropping to his knees, he fumbled around. Soft hair trickled across his hands.

April!

He'd found her!

He gave her a shake. No response. Desperate to escape the choking smoke and searing heat, he scooped her up and struggled down the endless walkway to the exit. He burst into sunlight and fresh air. God help him, he'd die if she didn't survive this. He needed her.

Something exploded behind him, knocking him to his knees. He staggered upright and, with both ranch dogs yapping at his heels, lurched farther away from the fully engulfed barn. When his strength gave out, he dropped to his knees and laid his precious burden on the ground.

He stroked April's hair back from her face and searched for a pulse.

"Ambulance is on its way," Jack offered in a panicky voice.

"She's breathing, but not by much. Her lungs must be full of soot." Wade leaned back, torn between fear and relief.

Together, they picked April up and moved her farther away from the heat.

Tommy skidded to a stop beside them on the quad. "What the hell? I saw the smoke from a mile away. Is she okay?"

"God, I hope so," Wade whispered, barely able to speak through his raw, scorched throat. "There's blood in her hair. Something must have hit her."

"Come on, boy, we've got to help Billy move animals," Jack said to Tommy.

The pig pen was close enough to risk damage from the fire. The goats, thankfully, were farther away. Unfortunately, the rabbit hutch was gone. They'd need to rebuild before Beth brought the rabbits over.

Neighbors roared in and started a bucket brigade. Not to stop the barn fire, but to soak down adjacent buildings and prevent the fire from spreading. The fire department would show up eventually, but the ranch miles from town, they would probably be too late. No fault on the firemen, time and distance were always factors when a decades-old building went up.

AFTER BEING TREATED for minor smoke inhalation and a couple small burns, Wade sat in the Edson hospital at April's bedside. A nasal cannula trailed from her upper lip, delivering precious oxygen to her damaged lungs. An IV tube fed into one arm and her head was swaddled in bandages. What he could see of her hair was brittle curls of burnt ends. And he'd never seen anything more beautiful in his life.

She was alive!

And so was he. He sucked in a relieved breath and started to cough. He covered his mouth until the spasms stopped, loath to wake her. She was fine, the baby was fine and being monitored, but they needed their rest and he had no intention of interrupting it. He sipped slowly at the water a nurse had generously provided him.

A soft touch stroked his bandaged arm where it rested on the bed.

Startled, he looked at April. "Hi," he croaked. "You're awake."

She mumbled something unintelligible.

Holding the cup in his bandaged hand, he used his uninjured arm to ease her up to take a drink. "Small sips, cowgirl."

She took a couple minuscule draws at the straw, then lay back down.

Leaning in he kissed her lightly on the cheek. "Thank God you're okay."

Wade pressed the buzzer and a nurse hurried in. She hustled him out of the room. He paced the hallway restlessly. A doctor came and went. Then another nurse. Still Wade paced until weakness overcame him and he dropped into a chair and promptly fell asleep. The past forty-eight hours since arriving at the hospital, had felt more like a thousand.

Tommy's voice woke him. "Wade? Wade? April wants to see you." Tommy shook him gently.

Wade blinked up at him.

"Yeah, man. Wake up." He held out a takeout cup. "Lukewarm coffee."

Wade gratefully swilled half the cup and cleared his throat. "Thanks."

"Hey, beautiful," he greeted April when he entered the room. He ignored the female RCMP officer standing on the far side of the bed, notebook in hand.

April chuckled weakly. "You look like hell, city-boy," she rasped.

"You're the most beautiful thing I've ever seen," he grinned, leaning down to kiss her cheek. "Thank God you're alive."

"I have some questions," the officer piped in.

"Can it wait?" Wade asked.

"Unfortunately, no. I know both of you are in rough shape, but it's been two days already. We need to get on with the investigation. So, Mr. Borne, what happened?"

"I don't actually know. I was away. I came back to the ranch. When I got there, the barn was on fire. Jack told me April had been inside and I went in after her." He ignored April's gasp. "The dogs led me to her. I carried her out. End of story."

The officer raised a skeptical eyebrow at him. "Just like that?"

"Just like that," he agreed.

"And why were you at the ranch? Don't you have a business in Calgary? A rather large business?" The question was pointed and almost accusatory. He reminded himself that she was just doing her job.

"I met April when I was on vacation. I stayed at the Lazy-W."

"But you left?"

Wade nodded.

"And you came back…why?"

It was a loaded question, and he knew it was designed to put him on the spot and make him feel uncomfortable. And it did, but not for the reasons the cop meant it to. It discomfited him more because he had innumerable things to clear up with April, confessions to make and plans to discuss, and she wasn't ready to hear all that.

"I'd rather not say."

"Mr. Borne, may I remind you that this is an official RCMP arson investigation and I can have you arrested for not answering my questions?"

"It's personal."

She quirked her eyebrow again.

"Talk to her," April whispered. "Please."

"I came back to convince April to give me another shot. To prove I'm not the asshole she thinks I am." Wade explained, not meeting the officer's penetrating look.

"Ah."

"Wade, you saved my life," April whispered, blinking away a tear and reaching up to touch his cheek. "You have your chance."

"So," the officer interrupted the moment between them, "you were in the barn, heard a voice, got hit in the head and woke up in the hospital?"

"That about sums it up," April agreed with a nod.

"Under other circumstances, it would seem suspicious, but Mr. Renault and Mr. Babiuk tell me you are on the up and up. In this case, I'm inclined to believe it."

"Who?" Wade looked back and forth between the cop and April.

"Jack and Tommy," April grinned. "You're their new hero. Jack, Mr. Renault, says you aren't so bad for a city slicker."

"I'll leave you two be. Although, there will be more questions. How can I reach you?"

Wade handed her a business card. "My cell phone would be the best choice, unless you feel I need my lawyer, then call the office. And be sure to check out Miller's reports on everything that's been happening out there. Something crazy is going on."

"I'll keep that in mind." She nodded, pocketed the card and then disappeared out the door.

CHAPTER TWENTY-SIX

*D*ay seven. April checked another box off her mental calendar. She never would have guessed she'd be in the hospital this long. Aside from seven stitches in the back of her head where she was struck, combined with the scorched hair and lung damage, she only had a few small burns to her arms. But, because of the baby, they were being extra cautious of her condition.

She'd been beyond fortunate that the arsonist, whoever he was, had set fire at the far end of the barn, and doubly fortunate Wade had finally come back to see her. She'd given up hope on him. She'd been certain the city had recaptured him.

April smiled to herself. Another day, another visit from Wade. Whatever the man's faults, he'd sure dedicated himself to keeping things going on the ranch until she got back on her feet. Thankfully, the doctor said she'd be well enough to leave the hospital in another two or three days. She was going stir crazy here. Today, they'd declared the baby safe and sound. Tomorrow she would be permitted to take short walks. No hard labor, no lifting or straining. But getting out of bed and walking further than the bathroom would be heaven.

She checked her watch. Seven a.m. and she'd been awake for two hours already.

Ranch chores were slowly getting caught up on, thanks to Billy and Tommy pitching in to aid Jack. However, despite all the hours she'd spent with Wade, there was still something tense and uncomfortable between them. There was so much more to discuss, but those conversations would have to wait until they were back at the ranch and less prone to interruption.

Until then, Wade came to visit every day for several hours. He told her he was working at the ranch but wouldn't disclose what he was working on. She anticipated and dreaded today's visit, but she might as well catch a few winks while waiting for him to arrive. A yawn overtook her.

She'd barely closed her eyes when soft footsteps sounded in the doorway. Not a nurse. She knew how they walked. She should after being here this long. Wade? Nope, wrong gait. The steps had a heavy masculine feel. Maybe a doctor.

The footsteps edged closer. A hard hand slapped down on her mouth, muffling her startled cry. Her eyes flew open.

Her uncle?

No way! She fought his tight hold.

"Stupid bitch," he snarled. "If you won't get off the damned land so I can sell it, I'll kill you here. The fire didn't get you, but I will."

His eyes were red and tortured. A crazy fever burned in

his expression. His skin was sallow. Deep, dirty wrinkles, like gouges, bracketed his eyes. He was filthy and stunk like garbage and unwashed filth.

"When you're dead, I'll come back and take what's mine."

Dead?

He yanked her pillow from under her head and slammed it onto her face, pushing down, trapping her against the rigid hospital mattress.

He was going to kill her!

Bucking and writhing, she struggled against him, her hands and legs flying everywhere. Nails scratching and digging wherever they found purchase.

He cursed and pushed down harder.

Spots appeared before her eyes and everything started to fade away. It became harder and harder to fight. She was going to die. She'd die without ever seeing her baby's face.

No!

With one final heave, using every ounce of strength she possessed, and the last air in her lungs, she jerked her knees upward and slammed into something solid. The pressure on her face eased a fraction of an inch and she wiggled over, just enough to slide off the far side of the bed.

She hit the nurse buzzer and staggered back against the window, leaning for strength and gasping for air.

"No," she gasped. "You can't hurt my baby."

"You've got a dammed brat?"

A bing sounded. "Nursing desk, what do you need?" a cheerful voice asked.

"He's trying to kill me."

An alarm rang and the room flooded with people as she

crumpled to the floor, unable to stand. She edged to her knees at the sound of flesh meeting flesh.

"Dammed asshole," Wade proclaimed shaking his fist and rounding the bed to help her up.

"Wade?"

"I knocked him out. Think I might have broken my hand in the process, but those nurses were no match for him. Here, let me help you get back into bed."

Gratefully, she grasped his other hand and levered herself to her feet. She grappled her way onto the bed and perched shakily on the edge, her arms wrapped around his waist, her head pressed into his belly. "Thank you," she whispered. "Is he done?"

"He is this time. We're taking him to the station. He won't be released anytime soon. There's no way he's seeing daylight after all of this," a cop who'd appeared out of nowhere proclaimed.

Hours later, Wade sat on the bed with his right arm wrapped around April's shoulders. His left hand was bruised but, thankfully, not broken. "They found the hospital security guard knocked out in the basement. He ID'd your uncle as his assailant. And you, my tigress, gave your uncle one hell of a bruise where you kneed him in the face. His cheek and nose are broken. That was one lucky hit."

"I had to save my baby."

"Nothing's more important than that precious cargo," he agreed and dropped a small kiss onto the top of her head.

She smiled at him. "No, but other things are coming close." The kiss was nearly her undoing. It sent ripples of emotion spilling out of her heart, straight to her tear ducts. She was so happy, so sad, so relieved. And Wade really did seem to care for her. Perhaps they could find a middle ground.

Two days since her uncle attacked her and finally, she was at home. April snuggled down into the couch and wrapped a quilt tightly around herself. Her new hand, Billy, had given it to her. He'd brought it when the dust settled. His mother, a woman April knew from her childhood, had sent it when she heard of the last attack.

Her uncle, John Wyatt, was locked up for psychological evaluation. The doctors said he was delusional and possibly certifiably insane. John believed his father was still alive and out to get him. The first step in any treatment would be to wean him off the cocktail of recreational drugs he'd been taking.

An updated version of the missing Will had been found in his backpack. Under better circumstances, everything would have been split equally between him and April. Under the terms of the new will, April's father had been left nothing, the stated reason being his wastrel ways and disrespect for April's safety and happiness as a child. As it stood now, Rex Tremble had ensured that April had full control over the ranch and any inheritance issues would be revisited after her uncle's trial. Provisions in the will stated that being convicted of a crime meant automatic disinheritance. Everything, the ranch, the equipment, the livestock, would go to April, except for a few minor donations to local organizations, including the 4H-Club. She'd yet to figure out where to find the money for that, but she would.

"If you're feeling up to it, we need to talk." Wade leaned against the living room door frame.

Her stomach plummeted to her knees. *Dear Lord, what now?* Hadn't there been enough problems, disasters and upheavals? Tempted though she was to bury her head under the blanket, she smiled weakly at him.

CHAPTER TWENTY-SEVEN

"We have to *talk*? Or, we *have* to talk?" she quipped, trying to lighten his serious expression. Was this it? Now that she had the ranch and her safety seemed assured, was he going to beat a hasty retreat back to the city? Hadn't they gotten close while she was in the hospital? She swallowed the lump in her throat. For a while, just before he left for his trip to the city, he seemed to be feeling something for her. It had been unsettling. She wasn't sure she wanted to feel anything for him in return. She almost laughed at that idea. She loved him. She'd fallen for him long ago. But there were so many logistical differences standing between them.

She was a country girl, through and through. He was all city, and a billionaire to boot. He'd never walk away from that and she'd never be happy in the city again. It had only just begun, but she was living a life here on the Lazy-W, one she wanted to make work. One where she relied only on herself.

"Kind of in between talk and *talk*," Wade suggested. "I have a confession to make. After that, we'll see where it goes.

So, when I was away in the city, I spent some time with Barbara. You remember Barbie?"

April nodded. Who could forget the porcelain cold heiress who had revealed Wade's identity? She was unforgettable in too many ways. The least of which was she'd been hooked up with Triad Resorts' attempt to gain the Lazy-W at a deep discount. If there was anyone April wanted to forget, it was Wade's ex.

"I didn't go 'see' her. But I did go visit Triad Resorts and she was there."

"Why would you go to Triad?" This didn't sound good. She was getting the sense of impending doom. She braced herself for an ugly revelation.

"I am, or rather, I was, a silent partner in Triad Resorts." He held up a hand. "I'm not any longer. Triad is owned by a friend. I loaned him some start-up capital years ago in exchange for partial ownership. Triad did all right by me. I've made a fortune off the deal. When I was there, having papers signed to turn my portion over for a payout, I bumped into Barbara. Literally."

Yeah, she was not liking where this was headed. It was headed south faster than a stampede of buffalo. And frankly, it smelled like manure.

"She was quite amused. She's dating Paul Paulson, owner of Triad now, and when Werner mentioned me being here, she wanted to tag along. She couldn't stop laughing at how she'd found me, accidentally, while helping her new beau find a location for a resort."

"How did she find out about the ranch?" This wasn't making any sense.

"She's got a drug problem. It used to be just a bit of grass every now and then, but by the time we broke up, she was doing more and continually drinking. Another reason she was wrong for me. Seems she ended up hurting herself and wound up in emergency. 'Some guy,' as she puts it, recognized her, from pictures in the newspaper, as Paul's girlfriend. He told her he knew of a mineral spring on land that might be for sale. Money changed hands and Triad started their research. I'm guessing the guy she bumped into was your ex. I talked to my investigator and it seems your ex was selling stolen drugs to your uncle."

"Hold on," she advised, burying her head in her hands. She needed to walk through this, slowly. His ex had met her ex, who was tied into drug dealings with her uncle, who was dealing through Miller's son…? The coincidences were almost unfathomable.

"Triad got impatient when they couldn't find John Wyatt and came to you. That must have been the last straw for your uncle. Warner told her I was here and she came out to mess with me. But that isn't what I wanted to talk about. Okay, it was part of it, but there is more." He raked his fingers through his sandy-brown hair. "I'm screwing this up. I had this all planned out in my head and I've fudged it up."

She watched his fingers clench and forearms bunch. Did any man, particularly a city slicker, have the right to such delicious muscles? She shook off the distraction. Tension radiated off him in waves; she could almost see it. His unease, his confusion comforted her. To see the imperturbable Wade Kelly Borne flustered was unthinkable. And if she admitted it, a little endearing.

"Relax, Wade. I'm not going anywhere. I'll listen to what you have to say."

His head jerked toward her, as if he'd forgotten she was there. For a second, he looked like he'd seen a ghost. A small grin wobbled at the corners of his mouth. He paced a bit more and finally paused in front of her, perching on the edge of the sturdy coffee table.

"I see now that what Barbra and I had was comfort and convenience, not love. When she started pushing for marriage, I realized she wasn't what I wanted in my life. I want, need, more than parties and business. Then there was her drug use and cheating. I broke up with her almost a year ago, but she kept hounding me. She's like a Pitbull on a pork chop. I couldn't stand it. I was burning out in business. It'd become overwhelming. I wanted out. That's when I packed a bag and left the city. To think.

"Since coming to the ranch, I've realized what I want. Companionship, trust, comfort. I want the whole damn ball of wax. I want to spend time with people who like me for who I am, not for what I can give them. And that, April Cooper, is you. You've shown me in a hundred ways that what I own doesn't matter. Who I am does. I'm a better man for meeting you. I love you, April Cooper."

The words were thrilling to hear, but not enough.

"It won't work, Wade. We're too different. Our lives are in different places. We live four hours apart. I'm not interested in a long-distance relationship. And I'm not leaving the Lazy-W. I have more than just me to consider. I have a child to raise." She placed her hand lightly on the growing bulge of her belly, comfort against the words that were an agony to push out. She wanted nothing more than to fall into his arms and find peace there, to confess her love. But she was a realist and a relationship between them would never work.

"You have a company to run and a charity who looks to you for guidance as well. You can't do that from here."

"Wrong."

His grin startled her.

"First, tell me that you love me too," he pleaded. "I've seen it in your eyes, felt it in the things you do. Admit it."

She pushed him aside and jerked to her feet, pacing the area he'd tread only minutes before. "It doesn't matter what I feel. A relationship between us is out of the question."

Wade rose and stepped in front of her, stopping her restless motion with gentle hands on her shoulders. "Look at me, April. Look at me and tell me you don't love me. If you can look me in the eyes and deny your love, I'll walk away and never look back."

Tears threatened. She blinked them back, staring at the floor until it came into focus. She was facing the hardest statement she'd ever made. She had to lie, with a straight face. To save her heart from further hurt, she had to lie to him. She'd made the wrong choice before. Settled with the wrong man, with a man whose priorities differed from hers. Wade was all business; she was hearth and home. The two ideals simply didn't mesh. So, she would lie. She'd tell him she didn't love him and he'd go away. A moment of pain now to avoid years of lingering heartache later.

Liar, if he leaves, I'll never get over him. Her heart cracked, but cracked was better than bruised and broken. She could do this; she could deny him.

She swallowed hard and looked up at him. He grinned at her. A silly, crooked, unsure grin.

She opened her mouth, closed it and swallowed again. "Wade Kelly Borne, I…"

His brows pinched together and his grin wobbled.

"I love you." The simple declaration startled her. It had been her intention to refute his claim.

"Whoop!" He threw his arms around her and spun her in a circle. "I knew it."

"You did not," she laughed. "I saw it in your face. You doubted me."

"No," he corrected. "*You* doubted you."

WADE WATCHED the laughter fade from her eyes as she looked at him. Now came the objections, but he had a plan to counter them.

"It won't work," she said. "I wish it would. But it won't."

"Hear me out." She was stubborn, there was no denying that. But he was more so. And his entire life, his happiness, was riding on convincing her. He was a negotiator, and he was good at it, the best; but he was facing his toughest negotiation. Ever.

"You've got a life in the city. Mine is here."

"My life in the city is done. Not entirely, but in three months, before our baby comes, I'll be retired. I'll be taking on a small roll at The Grace Foundation. That's the company I founded to help new businesses. It's from the money I inherited from my biological parents. It's the foundation that was and is prepared to give you funding to get this place back on its feet."

He smoothed the wrinkle between her brows. "I've done it all. I've travelled the world. I've made money, lost money. Screwed things up. But I'm not going to screw this up. I've had enough of the fast lane. Long before I found you stranded on the side of the road; I was looking for ways to pull back. WKB will be run by a board of directors with my closest friend Bronson Randolph as CEO."

Her frown faded slightly, so he went on. "It doesn't matter what happens here. Well, it does, but that's not what I meant. It's a done deal. Fini. Kaput. Stick a fork in it, it's done. The paperwork has been completed and recruiting for the new board has begun. So, even if you kick me off the ranch, I'm not going back to the rat race."

"Oh," she whispered, a hint of a smile playing at the corners of her mouth.

"It will require some sacrifices for both of us. No doubt I'll need to go to the city occasionally. I'll likely keep my apartment there. But you can come with me. We can go to shows, plays, the ballet. Hell, we can hang out in bars and drink tequila if that's what you want. But a few weeks of the year will need to be spent in the city, away from the Lazy-W. Can you handle that?"

"What about the baby?"

"That baby, your baby, my baby, is going to have the best of both worlds. Eventually, we'll have to get her a sibling or three."

"You'd care for another man's baby, just like that?" Doubt ricocheted off her words.

"How could I not. I'm the adopted foster child of two amazing people who took in a broken boy when his parents died. They raised me and loved me. They made me the man I am today. Family isn't who you're born to, it's who you love. That makes *you* my family. You and our baby, and even Jack."

April laughed, love blossoming and overcoming her.

Could it be true? Could it be that easy? Could they make this work? He was making so many sacrifices for her; would he come to regret them in the end?

"I won't regret it," he said. "I decided to cut free before I rescued you the first time. But being here, with you, has given me a new home, a new life." Certainty rang from his words. "I don't know much about ranching, but I'm one hell of a businessman. With our combined skills, we can't go wrong. We're going to turn the ranching community on its ear." He chuckled.

He leaned in and brushed his lips across hers. Lightly, but not tentatively. Their first real kiss. It felt like heaven. It felt right. She loved this man. Pressing forward, she returned his advance, deepening the kiss, wrapping her arms around his shoulders, threading her fingers in his hair. She showed him, without words, that she loved him right back. Eventually, they came up for air and he grinned at her.

"Oh yeah," he exclaimed. "One more thing."

He bolted out the front door and came back with a basket and placed it at her feet. "Since you're bringing a baby into this relationship, I thought it was only fair for me to bring one too." He reached into the basket and pulled out a tiny, wriggling Australian Sheppard puppy. "Meet Thyme. I adopted her from a nearby ranch. That took some doing, let me tell you. I had to prove I was worthy. If I hadn't dropped your name, I'd never have become the proud owner of an infant cattle dog. I called her Thyme, to fit the food theme of things here. If she'd been a male, I'd have called her Cash, because I parted with a pretty big sum to secure her. I'm pretty sure they took me to the cleaners with the price, but I don't mind."

"Oh, she's adorable." April dropped to her knees alongside Wade and Thyme, hugging them both close. "You really are serious, aren't you?"

"Dead serious. You stole my heart that day on the side of the highway and I've never looked back."

April rolled her eyes at the memory. Wade would never let her forget that embarrassing moment.

"April, will you marry us?"

Thyme leaped in Wade's arms, her slobbery tongue loving April's chin, echoing his question. This was it; this was what it was all about. Finding that one person who would do anything for you, who'd walk to the end of the earth to please you. The one who made your heart go pit-a-pat and made you jumpy and peaceful all at once.

"Yes, Wade. Oh, yes. I'll marry you."

Five crazy months had passed since they met. Today was their two-month anniversary. They'd wed quietly with only Wade's family, Herb and Beth, and the ranch staff in attendance. After a lot of talking and negotiating, Wade and April were partners now, in life, in the ranch.

"Now, don't get upset," Wade cautioned April as they passed the new barn on their way home from the hospital. The entire community, neighbors old and new had pulled together for an old-fashioned barn raising in early October, right after Wade and April's wedding. Wade pulled up in front of the ranch house. "I've invited some people over to meet our darling baby.

"Wade," she tried to sound chastising but ended up laughing. "How many? I don't see any cars."

"A few?" He winced as he parked beside the front deck. "You grab the little guy and I'll bring the car seat and the diaper bag. I'll get the rest of this paraphernalia after you're safely inside." He waved at the teddy bears and other gifts piled in the back. They'd only brought home one bouquet. They'd given the rest to the hospital staff to cheer up other patients.

Light snow drifted down around them. It wasn't going to amount to much, the forecast only called for half an inch, but it seemed a welcoming sight to bring their baby home to.

They climbed out of her brand-new Ford SUV and removed the sleeping baby from his car seat and stepped onto the porch. Thyme and two of the barn cats were cuddled up under the porch swing. They spared the returning family a brief glance and promptly returned to their slumber.

The living room was packed. Wade's adoptive parent's, Macy and Duke Birch, stood arm in arm. His sister, Micah, was there. Jack and Tommy stood in the background. Courtney, one of their first guests, was helping Beth and Herb Wood serve coffee. Half the neighbors were there, everyone eager to hold the baby. Aki, the vet, stood talking to their now permanent hand, Billy. His two adorable children could be heard playing in a bedroom.

Macy stepped forward and hugged the trio. "Welcome home, everyone. May I hold him?"

Without hesitation, April passed her three-day-old son over to the mother-in-law she'd grown to know and love over the past couple months.

"What are we going to call him?" Macy asked. "We can't keep calling him…him."

"Well," Wade affected a drawl. "After much consideration, we've decided to name him after me, April's grandfather and my father. He's gonna be a tough kid with all the opportunities in the world, so why can't he live up to three names? Everyone, say hi to Morgan Wade Duke Borne."

Everyone groaned at the mouthful of names for such a small boy.

"I like it," Duke, Wade's father, declared. "Suits him."

While everyone cooed over the baby, Wade and April slipped into the master bedroom.

"One more thing," Wade whispered, nuzzling her neck. "I have a small gift for the baby." Taking her by the hand, he led her into the bedroom they'd converted into a nursery. Instead of the store-bought crib she'd asked him to pick up, there was a beautiful hand-crafted crib.

"Oh, my gosh," she exclaimed, stroking the perfectly smooth, glossy spindles. "It's lovely. Where did you find it?"

"Jack and I built it. It's what I was working on while you were in the hospital all that time. I needed his help, a lot of it. But we did it together for you, and our baby. I needed to prove to you I was serious, that this is my life now. I wanted to remove all doubts you might have had about me."

She embraced him, tears of joy streaming down her face. "City-boy, I've loved you for eons. Even when I hated your interference, my heart was crying out for you. This is beautiful, but so unnecessary." She chuckled. "But I'm so glad you built this. For me. For us."

"I'm glad you like it. Now, before we rejoin our guest and claim our baby back. One last thing. For you."

"For me?" she asked quizzically. "I think that amazing crib is my gift. And our baby."

"Baby Morgan, my son, our son, is my gift. From you," Wade agreed. "But this one is just for you. I love you, April, more than I'll ever be able to explain." He pulled a small jeweler's box from his pocket and handed it to her.

"Jewelry? I already have this lovely wedding set." She

examined the delicate set of three rings they'd chosen together. Plain gold band, a band of alternating diamonds and garnets and a small diamond solitaire engagement ring. She adored the set, but more than that, she loved that he'd found them and that they suited her tastes so perfectly. She smiled up at him and opened the box.

Inside, nestled on a bed of red velvet was a delicate gold chain at the end of which was a glistening ball of polymer. April lifted it up and studied it. "Dandelion seeds?" She smiled. "How did you know?"

"You said it yourself, several times. Dandelions are drops of sunshine fallen from the sky. They turn into blow-flowers. Each blow-flower is a chance to make a wish. This is for you, *my* wish come true. A wish that will last forever, like our love."

"I love you, Wade Borne." She flung her arms around him and kissed him with every ounce of love in her heart.

"I love you, April Borne, future wife to all my children."

Love the novel you just read?
Your opinion matters.

Review this book on your favorite book site, review site, blog, or your own social media properties, and share your opinion with other readers.

Thanks in advance. Katie.

ABOUT KATIE O'CONNOR

Katie O'Connor lives in Calgary, Alberta, Canada. She married her high school sweetheart and is living her happily ever after. She is the mother of two grown daughters and is extremely proud of her five grandchildren. She has two wonderful sons-in-law and a large support network of friends, family and fellow authors.

Katie's career path has been long and twisted, with most of her life devoted to her family. She's been a waitress, chambermaid, cashier, store manager, as well as a lab and x-ray technician. She is an avid quilter and crafter.

She's dabbled in writing since high school because something drives her to create stories. She swears that it's impossible for her NOT to write. Unsatisfied with one genre, Katie writes contemporary romance, erotic romance and erotica. Recently, she's crafted her first cozy mystery with the intention of publishing a cozy mystery series.

She believes in all things magical; including dragons, fairies, UFOs, ghosts, and house pixies. But most of all she believes in love, romance and hope.

Katie likes to make it up as she goes along and dreams of publishing a mixed genre novel. It is going to be an erotic, shape shifter, vampire, steampunk, sci-fi, murder mystery, adventure, romantic, western, historical, thriller. It will be her biography.